CHOSEN BY THE VIKENS

INTERSTELLAR BRIDES®
BOOK 23

GRACE GOODWIN

SUBSCRIBE TODAY!

PATREON

$\mathcal{H}$i there! Grace Goodwin here. I am SO excited to invite you into my intense, crazy, sexy, romantic, imagination and the worlds born as a result. From Battlegroup Karter to The Colony and on behalf of the entire Coalition Fleet of Planets, I welcome you! Visit my Patreon page for additional bonus content, sneak peaks, and insider information on upcoming books as well as the opportunity to receive NEW RELEASE BOOKS before anyone else! See you there! ~ Grace

Grace's PATREON: https://www.patreon.com/gracegoodwin

GET A FREE BOOK!

JOIN MY MAILING LIST TO STAY INFORMED OF NEW RELEASES, FREE BOOKS, SPECIAL PRICES AND OTHER AUTHOR GIVEAWAYS.

http://freescifiromance.com

FIND YOUR INTERSTELLAR MATCH!

YOUR mate is out there. Take the test today and discover your perfect match. Are you ready for a sexy alien mate (or two)?

VOLUNTEER NOW!
interstellarbridesprogram.com

1

armen Andrianakis, Alias: Ms. Smith, Interstellar Brides Processing Center, Miami, Florida

Don't worry, she said.

Nothing will hurt, she said.

Only a formality...

Warden Egara was a liar. A brutal, cold, calculating...

"Look at me when I am fucking you, mate." The command plucked a chord inside my chest like my heart was a guitar string, and that damn string ran directly to my clit. Wet heat at my core throbbed and felt heavy. Empty.

No. Not me. Not *my* body. *Hers.* Whoever this stranger was, I was somehow locked inside her mind, feeling what she was feeling.

Wanting what she did. Needing it.

Like me, this woman had some sass. "You aren't fucking me yet. Not like he is."

Like he is? What?

Someone shifted beneath me, a massive cock moving in and out of my ass just enough to make me drop my head back and moan. God, it was so big. So tight. So, wicked, decadent, hot and... forbidden.

I clenched my muscles around that cock and forced a moan from the throat of the man beneath me. A feminine satisfaction I had never once felt in real life filled me like a drug. But this wasn't me. Right?

This body, this woman *knew* these men were hers and hers alone. There was no doubt. No shame. She laid on top of her lover, back pressed to his chest as he filled her from behind. As he plucked my—I mean *her* nipples. Growled in her ear. "You like that, mate? You want more?"

"Yes." The answer was immediate.

I—she—whatever. I was here. Somehow, I was experiencing what was happening to someone else's body. I had *two* lovers. One beneath me, holding me down as his hands played with my breasts, his cock buried inside me. The other stood before me, pre-cum leaking from the tip of his rigid length. My legs were spread wide. I was open and ready, so wet the air felt cold on my aching pussy.

Somehow I *knew* that he had just sucked me off, that his tongue and lips had worked my core, licked and sucked and devoured me until I exploded.

I *wanted* that cock inside me. Now. Right now.

Nothing less was going to satisfy me. I was an animal. Feral and needy. I'd heard the words *basic bitch* a thousand times and I was giving that stupid term a whole *new* meaning.

Lust was *basic*. Pleasure. I'd always dreamed about having more than one lover, but I'd never had the guts to try it out. I was an upstanding citizen. My momma took me to church every Sunday until I graduated from High School. I only had sex with someone I was dating and usually in the missionary position. I didn't ask for more. I never told the handful of lovers I'd had what I really wanted. Because what I dreamed about was naughty. Filthy. *Wrong*.

Here I was, naked with a cock inside my ass and another about to fill my pussy.

I felt *bad.* So, so bad. Naughty.

I wanted more.

As if this ghost woman read my mind, she arched her back, driving the shaft inside deeper even as I felt the wet lips of my pussy open like a flower. "Please."

The man before me cupped his cock, rubbing the pre-cum around the tip with his thumb. I looked up at him but couldn't quite make out his face.

Damn it, I wanted to see his—

"That's right, love. Beg." He thrust deep in one slow, smooth motion that had me keening like a wild animal. I was so close...

"Not yet, love. Don't you fucking come until you take all of us." A man's hand tunneled into my hair and angled my head back, my chin up and to the side. She gasped, but not in shock—as I was—but in anticipation. She *knew* this was coming.

I licked my lips and opened my mouth wide, reaching across the soft fabric for the muscled thigh I somehow knew would be there. He moved as I did, kneeling on one side of me, his foot placed on my opposite side, near my waist. There, easily within reach was a magnificent, massive cock attached to six-pack abs and thighs so muscled they couldn't be real. They just couldn't be—

I reached for his cock and pulled him down to me. Licked the tip to tease him.

"Fuck. Suck me down. Do it now."

As if for emphasis of that order, the two cocks buried in my body heaved forward to lift me closer. With a giggle that *never* would have come from my throat, she opened her mouth and took him throat deep in one go.

Holy shit.

"Now you may come, female. With your mates fucking you. You belong to us now."

Belong? I didn't belong *to anyone. I was not property. I—*

They moved. All three. Gently pulled back. Thrust deep.

Again.

They moved in rhythm as if they had done this a hundred times before. The hands on my nipples twisted just hard enough to burn but not hurt. The man fucking my pussy wrapped huge hands around my legs and held me open. The lover whose cock was in my mouth leaned over and took control of my wrists.

I was locked down. Trapped. There was nothing I could do but accept what they were doing to me. Take it.

Shame burned through me like wildfire through dry grass, but I couldn't stop because *she* would not stop. They fucked me over and over, all three of them touching me with hot skin. I could hear their breathing and mine. Frantic. Out of control.

She didn't feel any guilt or remorse. She had no second thoughts. She took them as if it was her right to feel this way, to want them all, to fuck them all.

God. I couldn't imagine. But now I didn't have to.

The orgasm roared through me like a freight train at full speed and I cried out around the cock in my mouth. My pussy and ass muscles clenched down, the tightness, the resistance making the muscle spasms inside me even stronger. There was a sharp sting as one of them gave a light swat to my bottom. It was perfect.

Yes... I was exploding into glitter. Burning to ash. There was nothing left of me but their cocks. Their hands. Emotion surged through me like a flash flood of joy. Lust.

Love.

Shit. That last one was *definitely* not me.

"Ms. Smith? Can you hear me?" The question was from a female voice, not Kayson. The confusion pulled me away from my lovers. Their hands. Their cocks.

Nooo. The love the woman had for her lovers overwhelmed me like a dagger to my chest. My eyes burned. Tears rolled freely down my cheeks. It hurt. So bad.

"Ms. Smith? The testing is over. How are you feeling?"

Testing? I was taking a test?

"I know it is difficult, but you need to let go. Don't fight the program."

Program? I tried to blink. Focus. Nothing felt right. Or real.

"Ms. Smith? Can you hear me? You are at the Interstellar Brides Processing center. I am Warden Egara. We just completed your planetary assessment required to clear you for your mission." A small, cool hand rested against my cheek for a moment, then my forehead.

"Yes. I can hear you." Damn it. *Mission.* One word and it all came flooding back to me. I sounded like I'd eaten half a can of nails and not yet recovered. Smith wasn't my real name, but I wasn't sharing that bit of information either.

"Excellent."

"Water."

"Of course." I blinked the woman into focus as she used a nod of her head to order someone to bring me water. At least, that's what I *thought* she was doing. I'd get the water myself, but I was strapped down to a chair that looked like it belonged in the horror story version of getting a tooth pulled. Of course, any trip to the dentist was a nightmare for me. Total nightmare.

I laughed at myself. Idiot. I could be shot at by international criminals and mercenaries without batting an eye. Put me in a dentist's chair and I needed laughing gas and a sedative.

Ironic. That was the word I was looking for.

"Ms. Smith. The water?"

I brought myself back to the room and found one of Warden Egara's minions holding a small plastic cup full of water to my lips. Grateful, I leaned forward and did my best to drink it as she poured. In the end, I only had a few drops soaking the chest area of my processing gown. I considered that a win.

"Thanks."

"Of course." The young women smiled at me briefly before nodding at the warden and exiting the room. The finality of the locking noise I heard when the door closed had my hands in fists. Here we go.

"Well?" I leaned forward as far as the wrist bindings would allow. "Did I pass your little test?" I was the fifth agent they'd brought here for this assignment. The first four women had never come back.

"Indeed. You are the first to be compatible with Viken."

"Great." I'd passed. Now she could get on with this— "What do you mean, I'm the first? What happened to the other four agents? They never reported back. I assumed they went to Viken as well."

"Oh, no." Warden Egara smiled at me like I had missed the punchline of some joke.

"Then why didn't they come back?"

"They accepted their matches and left Earth behind to claim their mates."

"They what?" Was this a bad joke? "I knew Agent Spinoza. She never would have abandoned her job like that. No way."

"Maria Spinoza was matched to Trion and completed her processing and transport yesterday. I am sure her mate has claimed her by now."

"On Trion?" I'd heard of the planet. I'd been debriefed on *all* the various alien civilizations and their... lifestyles. I tried to imagine my friend, Maria, tied up and helpless as a massive alien's big cock slammed deep.

My pussy did a little dance inside me. Again. The idea of being tied up turned me on almost as much as the three on one sex-capade I'd experienced in my own processing test.

The warden smiled. "She was a ninety-six percent match."

Of course she was. Jeez. I wondered what percentage success the magic matching machine—alien computer—had given my match to Viken. I opened my mouth to ask, then stopped. No. I didn't want to know. The less I knew the better.

Didn't matter how hot my fellow agents turned out to be. Absolutely didn't matter that I was going to have to pretend to belong to three aliens on one of the most primitive -minded planets I'd ever heard of.

Semen that makes a woman crazed and obsessed with having *more sex*? Yeah, I'd read the brief on Viken.

Society. Biology. Everything the agency had on them—and it was a lot. I'd pored over every detail. Committed it to memory.

These aliens were going to be keeping their jizz to themselves. I wasn't staying...

2

*K*ayson, *Royal Guard, Viken United, The Palace Medical Wing*

I PACED the long medical wing's corridor, my heart heavy with guilt. The queen, my beloved leader and longtime friend, sat at her daughter's bedside. The little princess, Allayna, lay unconscious in the healing pod, her perfect skin like milk, her auburn hair a halo around her face.

I couldn't help but feel responsible for the child's injuries. It was my duty, along with my fellow guards Mal and Geros, to protect the royal family from harm, and yet we had failed. This was the fourth attempt on the princess's life in a matter of weeks. I had overheard this time she had come close to dying amidst a sea of blood. A knife wound to her lung had barely missed her heart, and the doctors did not know if she would ever wake from the coma created by the healing pod.

The queen looked up at us, her eyes filled with fury and determination. "I will not let them harm my child again," she said, her voice wavering with emotion. "I have summoned you three here for a new assignment."

"Your highness," I replied, bowing my head in shame. "We are deeply sorry for failing to protect Allayna."

"I understand your feelings," she said, "but now is not the time for apologies or self-loathing. This might be my last opportunity to save my daughter. As queen it is my duty to protect all of Viken and its people, but I can't do that if I am unable to protect my own family."

"Anything, my queen." I dipped my head, the respect I had for her real, not feigned.

"Your majesty, we will do whatever it takes to protect Allayna and put an end to these attempts on her life." Geros confirmed my feelings on the matter. This threat would be dealt with, one way or another.

"I know you will do whatever it takes. That is why I have summoned you and no others. No one is to know what I am about to tell you. No one except myself and the three kings. Do you understand?"

When Geros, Mal and I had all agreed, she rotated her shoulders back and stretched her neck, the hours of silent vigil at her daughter's side clearly taking their toll. "I know you are honorable males. Loyal and worthy. I am tired of waiting for the investigation to go through the proper diplomatic channels." She looked over at the little princess and her lips thinned in a severe line. "I am tired of waiting for Viken politicians to take care of my problem. That's why I have summoned a special agent from Earth to work with you. She is an expert at infiltration and finding criminals who don't want to be found."

"Excuse me? Did I misunderstand? You summoned a *female* from Earth to hunt the leader of the most vicious and lethal threat to Viken?" Mal's tone was not approving. The queen glared at him in response.

"Yes. And I expect you three to treat her as if she were me."

Geros inclined his chin even as Mal crossed his arms and scowled. Typical for both of them, but it was Geros who spoke. "Why? I do not understand what a small female from your home world can do to assist the trained guards already hunting our enemies."

The queen smiled and I felt my skin go cold. "Are you familiar with snakes? The Cobra? Rattlesnake? Black Mamba?"

"No." That was Mal, straight and to the point. "You know we are not. Those are from your world. We do not have such creatures on Viken."

"Oh, but you do." The queen said the name of a long, silent predator native to our world that used venom to paralyze its prey before swallowing it alive.

"Yes, it has been years since I saw one." Geros was the one who answered her and his voice did not betray anything of his thoughts. "It was a young male, barely as long as I stood tall. It was eating the seabird eggs on the southern shore."

"What has this snake creature to do with the human female, or the VSS?" That was Mal, again, painfully direct.

"The humans have a saying: If you go after the king, you go after his entire court."

"That is an Earth saying. And it has nothing to do with snakes."

"It is a perfect description of what is happening here. The kings, my daughters, we are all in danger. I cannot blast open the doors of the VSS and demand their heads. I need someone who can sneak in undetected and paralyze my prey. And that, gentlemen, is why I have sent for her."

"We are the explosives and this human female is your snake?" Geros asked.

"I do not disagree with your assessment, but you know that I do not like this," Mal growled. "I cannot stand by and allow a female to be harmed."

Viken warriors were raised to be both protective and aggressive, fiercely loyal to their mates. I had no issues with any of that, but I had serious doubts about this small human being able to accomplish the task Queen Leah had set before her. I also agreed with Mal. It was not in our nature to do what the queen was asking of us.

"I am your queen. You will obey me. Once she arrives, everyone except the kings and I will believe she is your true matched mate. In private, she is a colleague. Nothing more. You are not to touch her. In public, you will behave as if she is your mate. No one must suspect our ruse or the entire plan may fail."

"Our mate?" Mal's brows tightened and he was shaking his head. "No. How can we convince anyone this female is ours and not be allowed to touch her?"

"How much you will be allowed to touch her in public is her decision. She will guide you. You will remember at all times that she is *not* your mate. You will honor this female and assist her in any way you can. She is in charge of this mission, not you. And I assure you, placing herself in danger is her specialty." Queen Leah looked extremely pleased with herself. Sending a female to us that was not our own, one that we must protect but not touch?

Gods be damned. What level of torture were we to endure? We had all been tested for the Interstellar Brides' program. We'd all been waiting for years. And now we must endure this? To be so close. To live with a female who was not ours. To cherish and dote on her in public and immediately cease in private?

"I'd rather fight the Hive," Mal mumbled. I didn't disagree. This mission was going to torment all three of us.

The queen ignored his comment. "As news of *any* new Interstellar Bride's arrival on Viken travels quickly, we must keep up appearances from the second she appears. She will complete the transport as any standard bride.

She will be naked. You will immediately move to cover and claim her, as if she were your true mate."

Fuck. It was even worse than I'd imagined. Naked? *Pretend* she was ours when we had already been waiting years for a matched mate? A female to cherish. And touch. And taste.

An order was an order. The queen was not a woman you disobeyed, and not simply due to her rank. She inspired loyalty. The people of Viken, outside of the VSS, not only adored her, they loved her for giving us our heir, the one who would truly unite the three sectors after decades of war. Princess Allayna. Allayna's younger sister, the charming princess Lilliana, with her golden hair and bouncing curls—apparently inherited from the three kings' grandmother—was equally treasured. The tiny princess could not yet speak clearly, but she could smile and babble, and that smile had stolen everyone's hearts.

I glanced at Allayna once more, at her unmoving little body in the pod. Were that my daughter, I would have torn the entire planet apart to hunt her attackers.

We would do what needed to be done.

I exchanged quick glances with both Mal and Geros. Both gave nearly imperceptible nods. We would accept this assignment. And I would hope against hope that the female sent to us was the most heinous looking hag in the history of females. Somehow, I doubted we would be so lucky.

3

*M**al, Transport Room*

THERE WAS no arguing with the queen. As much as I hated the situation, I could not fault her logic. Everything our investigators had tried had failed. We needed a new approach. And no one on Viken would suspect a female of such treachery.

I found my curiosity high as I waited to see what kind of mate we would be dealing with. To be worthy of this assignment, she must be large and muscled more like a male than a female. Viken culture celebrated softness and submission in its females. They were not trained for war or hunting. Not because they were not capable, but because we could not overcome our fierce need to protect and provide. It was deeper than cultural, it was instinct. We were born to cherish and care for our females.

Everything about this situation was wrong.

Kayson and Geros stood looking as uncomfortable as I felt. The queen stood beside us as well. And she was correct. Gossip and rumor of a new bride's arrival had traveled throughout the island of Viken United. Luckily our home was small, with only the palace and offices, homes and basic markets for the those who worked in our government. Perhaps a thousand people lived here and I would bet half of them lined the halls and streets beyond this room, eager to see our new mate.

Our false mate. The 'snake' sent from Earth to sneak into the dark places of this world. She was to arrive at any moment.

"This is so exciting. I can't wait to have another friend from home to talk to." The queen clapped her hands together and smiled as if she didn't have a care in the world. I did not understand human females. Mere moments ago, she'd wiped tears from her eyes as she promised Allayna she would be back.

Once before we had encountered a human female. She had been upset with her mates. Nearly inconsolable. I had very much wanted to keep her, but she had done what a true matched mate would do. She chose to return and claim her males.

I had never forgotten her. I had even dreamed of having a mate from Earth. But this?

Fuck. This was the worst idea in the history of bad ideas.

My body's needs had not been fed in many months. And now I was to stand by as an unclaimed female hunted *our* enemies? Pretend she was mine? Cherish her one moment and send her directly into danger the next?

I was so fucked.

The hum of energy filled the transport room as the officers at the control panel confirmed a visitor was about to arrive. And then...she did.

My worst nightmare had come to life. The naked female lying unconscious on the transport pad was beyond beautiful. Her face was perfectly symmetrical, with a strong jawline, high cheekbones, and a straight nose. Her skin was smooth and had a warm tone. She had dark, arched eyebrows and long, curled lashes.

I wondered if her eyes would be large and dark or a pale hue. My gaze caught on full lips that looked softer than a flower petal. Immediately my mind imagined tasting them, watching those lips close around the head of my cock.

"Fuck. This is not going to work." I was already hard as a rock, every thought consumed with claiming her.

"And why is that, Mal?" The queen raised a brow and tapped one foot, as I had seen her do with her mates when she was annoyed.

I tore my gaze from the female on the transport pad and met the queen's slightly irritated look. She glanced from me to the officers working the transport controls and I realized my blunder. Still, I could not lie to my queen.

I hid nothing of my carnal thoughts, nor did I hide the prominent bulge of my hard cock. "You know why. Perhaps you should choose someone else."

This female was not ours to keep. I had known the mission would be difficult. Now, having seen her, I knew it would be painful as well.

"I trust no one else and neither do my mates." Queen Leah shrugged. "I suggest we save that conversation for later, gentlemen. I believe your mate is stirring."

The human female would not welcome our touch. She did not want us, any of us. We had not been matched. All of this was nothing more than a ruse. That knowledge did nothing to deter any of us from scrambling to her side. We were supposed to act as real mates would. Treat her as if she were truly our matched mate, as everyone on the planet must believe, if the queen's plan had a chance to work.

If she were mine, she would already be in my arms, wrapped in the softest blanket I could find as I carried her to our new shared quarters. Once there I would run my fingers through the long, ink-black fall of silken hair and breathe the scent of her skin deeply into my lungs. I would taste her everywhere. Touch her everywhere. Fuck her until she was a sobbing, exhausted mess. Then I would curl around her like a protective shell and order her to sleep so I could do it all again.

But she was not our mate. Not Kayson's. Not Geros's. And not mine.

Not fucking mine.

She was here on a mission to track down assassins and killers. Once that mission was complete? She would leave Viken behind and return to Earth. She was not an Interstellar Bride. There were no laws in place that would keep this beautiful female with us.

Gods be damned, that didn't stop my cock throbbing in pain as I took one more look at her soft curves. Her full lips. She was small, much smaller than any of us. Her muscles were well-honed with long, toned legs. Her waist curved above her hips to...her breasts were round... *oh fuck*, I wanted to suck on them until she bucked and begged.

I bowed my head and closed my eyes for a count of ten to gain control of myself. I'd seen enough to recognize that her muscles were roped with power. She was not weak, as I'd feared. That strength would make her surrender all the sweeter.

I watched Kayson's hand fly to his cock, readjusting it through the leather uniform pants he wore, as he gazed upon our new mate. He wanted her, too. He shifted his hips, and the thin material of his uniform pants tightened, outlining his erection. The queen's gaze landed on the bulge in his pants. Her attention drew Geros's eye as well.

Geros sighed and shook his head as we both knelt down on the transport pad next to our not-mate. "This mission is going to be fucking impossible." He whispered the words so only I would hear them. I did not disagree.

"She's not meant to be ours, Geros." I clenched my hands into fists as Kayson knelt down as well. We formed a protective circle around the female and Kayson placed a soft blanket around her shoulders.

The light touch woke her up. Her eyes fluttered open.

Brown. Dark, warm brown.

She grabbed onto the edges of the blanket and pulled it tightly around her body like a cocoon. The action covered her soft breasts. Her long, smooth legs. The smallest hint of her pussy. All were hidden now, but it was too late. The sight had already been burned into my mind.

We were to act as if she were truly ours. One glance at the officers operating the transport controls and I realized that meant starting right fucking now. So I did what I wanted to do, what I would have done without hesitation, if she were mine.

I picked her up in the cradle of my arms and drew her close to my chest. I nestled her hair with my cheek, inhaling her soft feminine scent.

She relaxed against me and the question of whether it was a true reaction to me or all for show consumed me.

She'd been here a matter of minutes and I was already losing my mind.

I closed my eyes and breathed deeply. Her scent hit me harder now. My hunger to bend her to my will grew restless. I could feel the need stirring on the inside. To

conquer. To dominate. To serve her and bring her pleasure. To earn her trust so she would fully submit. Now
that I'd seen her, the need woke within me and roared
like a monster. I had been too long without a female.
Perhaps I should soothe that itch before we left for the
city.

No. Even the thought revolted me. I didn't want
another female. I wanted her.

She was an undercover agent from Earth, sent to infiltrate a terrorist organization that threatened our entire
planet. I repeated this information over and over in my
mind. I was not supposed to want her, but I did. Badly.

I opened my eyes to find her gazing up at me. Assess-
ing. Taking my measure.

"Bring your mate and follow me to the conference
room." We followed her like small children behind a
teacher "Ms. Smith, I hope you can forgive me but I am
so excited to see another human. When I heard you were
coming, I danced with Allayna for an hour. Let's just say, I
am eager to talk to you." The queen glanced at the transport officers, who chuckled at her girlish tone.

She had them all fooled. The entire planet had no
idea just how serious Allayna's injuries truly were. Nor
did they know the little princess was still unconscious in
a ReGen pod. They didn't need to know. Just like they
didn't need to know the female in my arms didn't belong
to us. Wasn't a true bride.

The female tore her wide-eyed gaze from mine and I
immediately felt adrift. Her voice filled the corridor, the

sound like a hand wrapping around my cock. "Of course, Queen Leah. I would love to get the native's tour."

"Just Leah." The queen smiled. "Out here, us Earth girls stick together."

"Just Leah, I don't use the Ms. Just call me Smith." Smith smiled then, and it was beautiful. How had she come to be here? With us? Any true male of worth, on Earth or any other planet, would have been hard pressed not to desire her. Fuck her. Claim her. Were human males such idiots?

They must be.

Smith shifted in my arms, her softness moving over my chest and abdomen. The contact was startling. Intimate. Did she know the effect she had on me? How could she?

"I need to, uh...get dressed first?" She looked at the queen. "I would love to talk to you, but I don't want to do it naked unless I absolutely have to."

Queen Leah laughed—the first time I'd heard the sound since the latest attack on Allayna—and Smith earned my gratitude if nothing else.

"Of course. Your mates will take you to your quarters." The queen looked at each of us in turn, her gaze direct and saying what she wouldn't say aloud. *Treat her like you would treat me. She is in command of this mission. Respect. Obey. Do not touch.* "Get a good night's sleep. Transport from Earth can be exhausting. They will give you anything you'd like to eat. All of Earth's most popular dishes have been programmed into the S-Gen machines. Just ask and it will be yours. We can talk tomorrow."

"Wow. Thank you. Warden Egara didn't ask for my size. Do you need that to get me some clothes?"

The queen grinned at the newest, clueless human to arrive on our home planet. "No, Ms. Smith. I do not. They have marvelous machines here that will scan your body and make custom clothing for you on the spot. Any style you want. Gowns. Uniforms."

"Are you kidding?"

"Shoes, too."

"Shoes?"

Leah's voice dropped despite our private surroundings. "As well as weapons."

"Holy shit."

That made the queen chuckle. "I know, right?"

Smith grinned. "Good. I was dreading running around without my Glock."

"We have much better firearms than that out here. I'll have your mates give you a list of available weapons as well as show you how to use them, if you'd like?"

"Oh, hell yeah. That would be great."

I did not like the fact that the military lock on the S-Gen machine's weapon's security access had been removed for Smith. No. I didn't want to imagine this soft female with a weapon in her hand, facing down someone who wanted to hurt her. Kill her. Not one bit. Nor did I have any intention of placing one of our extremely dangerous ion blasters into her hands.

"Geros, see to it."

"Yes, my queen."

Fuck. The queen must have known I wouldn't do it. Of course she did. I had forgotten how observant and cunning our three kings' mate truly was.

And if this stunning creature in my arms was anything like her, we were all going to be in trouble.

4

eros

I WALKED behind our queen and Mal, who was carrying Smith to our new quarters. Kayson kept pace on my right and I remained on high alert until the queen had wished us a good evening. Once inside our new quarters, Mal had--reluctantly--placed Smith on her feet. She still wore nothing but the blanket. Knowing she was naked beneath was not helping any of us remain calm.

We had to work with her for the next few weeks. Get to know her. And keep our hands to ourselves. But fuck, that last part was going to be like holding sweets in front of three big babies and telling them not to eat.

Never had I seen a woman as beautiful as Smith.

Everything about her was soft. Feminine. Her eyes, her lips, her neck, her collarbone and her breasts... fuck, her breasts. The curve and color of them were the perfect. They were not too big, nor were they too small. They were perky, the areolas small and puckered. She was pale, but not with a deathly pallor--rather, she had a healthy glow and luster that made her radiant. Smith was beautiful. And I wanted to keep her.

Smith watched us. We tried not to stare at her as she looked around our new and very private quarters. The room was bigger than anything we'd had before; two bedrooms and a large living area. The S-Gen machine was in the corner between the dining table and living area. I noticed, not displeased, that the sofa was more than large enough for all four of us.

Smith held onto the edge of the blanket, clutching it to her chest. She held her ground as we approach, forming a loose semi-circle around her. This was the first time we had all been alone. I wondered if she was nervous or afraid. I wanted to reach out and hold her, but that was not my place.

I watched as she tried to make sense of the room and the technology, which I was sure she had never seen before. To her credit, she was not shaking nor showing any outward sign of distress. If not for the rapid pulse at the base of her neck, I would have believed her completely unaffected by her adventure. She traveled across the galaxy to work for a queen she had never met. Would now pretend to be mated to three experienced warriors who wanted to strip that blanket from her shoulders and show her ultimate pleasure. And yet she stood commandingly before us, seemingly calm and in control.

It appeared she wanted to talk. "So you three are the lucky ones, huh?"

"Indeed." Mal's sour countenance was not going to win her heart anytime soon.

"Do you guys take on a lot of missions like this?"

"This is the first." Kayson perched on the arm of the sofa, I suspected so he would not appear so tall. This human female was delicate and small. It would not do to frighten her.

"And the last." Mal nearly growled the words. I expected her to be offended. Instead, she grinned.

"You, too? I don't want to be here either."

Her words shocked me. "Then why are you here?"

She walked around the edges of the room slowly, taking it all in, lightly running her fingertips over furniture and trinkets. There was not much, as this was a new space designed for matched mates to live. The majority of the decorative choices were generally left to those who would live there. Permanently.

"The usual." She answered but did not turn. Avoiding eye contact.

So...not completely unaffected.

"I assure you, what may be usual on Earth will not be the same here." Kayson spoke softly, but it was clear he wanted further explanation.

"Oh, it is. This is the same everywhere. Honor. Duty. Service. Following orders. Plus, if I pull this off, my boss has promised me a new position and a lot more money."

"A promotion?" I asked. We understood that term. Higher rank. More power and more responsibility. This female must be regarded highly to be given such a delicate mission.

"Why does your boss care what happens here?" Mal moved toward her, a scowl on his face.

"He doesn't. He cares about the queen of Viken owing him a personal favor."

Mal reached her side and loomed over her. Instead of shrinking away, she stood boldly, face to face, even though she had to tilt her head nearly as far back as it appeared to be able to go.

"What? You don't like working with a woman?"

"I adore females."

"I'll bet you do."

"What are you implying?"

"You heard me. I bet you are used to being fawned over and flirted with everywhere you go."

I couldn't help it, I choked on a short burst of laughter. She wasn't far off. Everywhere we went, females took one look at Mal, his piercing blue eyes, black hair and square jaw and somehow, they just *knew*. They watched him with hungry eyes; created excuses to speak to him. They cried in frustration when he did not return the attention.

He was oblivious to them all. He hadn't always been,

but he'd gone dark recently. Spent more and more time alone. He seemed to have no interest in females at all.

He was a Master Dominant at Club Trinity in Central City. It was one of the reasons—no, the only reason—the queen had chosen us for this mission. Sure, she said she didn't trust others to handle the task, but I was not a young fool born yesterday. I knew flattery when I heard it. There were dozens of guards here who would die to protect the royal family without hesitation. But Mal's status at the club where the suspected traitors operated would get us inside.

Would get *her* inside.

"And you are not fawned over and flirted with on Earth? Pursued?"

"No. Me? Are you kidding? I'm way past my college days, I eat too many sweets—and it shows on my hips— and as soon as a man finds out what I do for a living, he runs hard and fast in the opposite direction." There was bitterness in her voice, and regret. She'd been hurt before over this *job* she performed, by stupid males. Perhaps both.

"What do you do for a living?" Kayson was probably trying to break the tension between Mal and Smith, but it didn't work. "Why would any male run away from you? You are very small, not a threat."

She grinned, at least, and her tone softened a bit. "I disappear for months at a time. I go deep undercover. I don't have a life. I have one plant that has managed to survive because it's a cactus. I don't even have a goldfish.

I'm married to my work. That's why." She took a step away from Mal and tilted her head to the side. "Why are we doing this? We have to pretend to like each other, remember?"

"I remember," Mal said. Oh fuck yes, all three of us *remembered* just fine.

"I'm sorry. This has been one hell of a week. I shouldn't take it out on you guys. Not your fault." The sass in her eyes faded to sadness and I wanted to shoot Mal with my ion blaster for the change. "I'm just tired. And naked. And that transport thing hurts like a son-of-a-bitch. Egara didn't give me a heads up on that one. Would have been nice."

I stared. She wasn't making sense, but seeing this side of her—hurting and tired and speaking truth to us? I had to sit down next to Kayson to stop myself from touching her. Holding her.

She sighed. "Don't get me wrong, I haven't changed my mind. And the promotion will be nice." She put an odd, geometric shape back on a ledge, the object meant to be soothing to the eye.

"But?" Kayson asked.

She broke eye contact with Mal to turn toward Kayson. "I don't like bad guys who hurt little kids. I've seen enough of that back home. If I could, I'd burn every one of those bastards alive."

The breath left my body as if I'd been kicked in the chest. By the gods, she would be a fierce and protective mother.

She tore her gaze from Kayson and looked at me. "So, tell me about this club we are going to. Tell me everything, so I know what I have to do."

Mal moved slowly and tipped her chin up with a gentle touch. "Surrender. Trust me with your body. Tell me your secrets. Let me see inside your soul so I can give you what you need."

"Oh, is that all?" Her whispered response held a hint of laughter.

My cock grew into a painful bulge in my pants as I imagined Mal pulling the blanket from her body. I would hold her in my arms and take her from behind.

Fuck her. Touch her. Kayson and Mal would do the same. Be one. Be together. Make us a real family.

But that wasn't why she was here.

Mal did what only he could do. He asked her intimate questions about things she would not have shared under any other circumstances. I listened, trying and failing not to show too much interest.

Several times she paused and I saw the lie in her eyes. The hesitation. She was keeping secrets.

Much later I watched her disappear down the hallway. My cock throbbed painfully with need. The musk of her wet pussy filled my senses, pulling me to her. I'd smelled her heat. The conversation with Mal had not left her unaffected. Her pussy had been wet for the last hour. She'd stumbled over her words as the sweet scent taunted me. Called to all three of us.

I wouldn't sleep this night. I wouldn't even try. Not

when she would be so close to us in our quarters. Not when I could catch a scent of her and want to kiss the skin at the curve of her neck. Her breasts. Taste her wet heat. Hear her cries of pleasure.

Not when she was so close, and yet so far away from all of us.

5

eros, Central City, Club Trinity, Two Days Later

MAL and I walked into the BDSM sex club, our *mate*, Smith, sheltered between us. I looked at her smooth hair and wanted to touch. The soft skin beneath the sheer red gown she wore did little to hide her pert breasts, curved hips or her perfect, round ass.

I lifted my gaze to the full-length mirrors placed strategically along the walls. Captivated by her entrance, I watched her move. My cock throbbed in response to her sensual walk as she followed Mal to the security desk.

Club Trinity was the most famous BDSM club on the planet and security was tight. According to Mal, anyone stupid, or lucky enough to get past security would be met with a room full of Doms who would kill to protect the subs under their care. This place was a fortress and a safe house. Which was probably why the VSS had chosen to hide within its walls.

"Master Mal. We have not seen you here in some time." The male guarding the entrance to the exclusive back rooms of Club Trinity recognized Mal instantly. Had Kayson or I tried to walk into the exclusive areas of the club, we would have been escorted to the door with blasters in our backs.

Smith stood between us looking radiant, as a new bride should. We were going to take her inside, tie her down and make her scream with pleasure. She just didn't know it yet.

The male lifted the small scanner attached to the inside of his forearm and pressed it to the side of Mal's wrist, where his three-headed serpent tattoo had been etched into his skin. The colorant used contained something the club owners could scan to verify authenticity. Many tried to fake the mark; only Master level dominants were allowed to have them.

He completed the scan and nodded at Mal. "I believe all of your requests have been met, Sir. If you require anything at all, we are at your service."

When the guard was done speaking, he lowered his arm and pressed the button hidden somewhere behind his impenetrable cube. A large buzz and click indicated the door was opening. It slid wide and I tried not to stare at the reinforced metal nearly as thick as my thigh. No one was getting through that door with anything less than a ship- sized ion blaster.

"Thank you." Mal placed his hand at the small of Smith's back and led us deeper into the club.

We walked past the noise and chatter of the main area via a side hallway that most of the patrons seemed to ignore. We reached the end of the barren stretch and stood before another door, this one black with the three-headed serpent symbol embossed in gold at shoulder level. Two guards stood at this door.

Mal stopped and took his time removing Smith's cloak, as if unwrapping a treasure. The red fabric of the negligee beneath was nearly translucent with nothing more than a small string covering her ass. Another thin strip of red held her breasts up, the nipples prominent and yet not quite as easy to discern under both layers of seductive clothing. With a slight nod at Mal, one of them took Smith's cloak. The other opened the door and stepped aside so we could enter, each looking with open hunger at our female.

Mal ignored them, although I could have sworn he clenched his jaw. She was beyond beautiful and Mal had explained to all of us that the Dom's in Club Trinity loved to show off their submissives almost as much as the subs enjoyed taunting the other Dom's with what they could not touch.

Smith showed no reaction. I had to admire her spirit. This was no place for the faint of heart. The moment the door clicked and locked behind us, I heard the first moan of pain. The crack of a whip. A submissive male begging his Dom to fuck him. From the look of anticipation on the face of the giant male standing over his sub, they were just getting started.

The main area here was smaller but slightly better lit than the former rooms of the club. The music was at a lower volume. Less wild party and more relaxing. We moved through the sparse crowd, which parted as we passed.

Mal stopped before one of the plush sofas lining the walls of the room. A uniformed male stood the moment he saw Mal. He approached, smiling and extending an arm in welcome.

"Mal. I saw your name on the list for tonight and thought I was hallucinating. But here you are."

"It's good to see you, Doyle."

Mal and Doyle clasped forearms. Doyle did not ask about me or Smith, but Mal was not rude nor forgetful. Had Doyle been a stranger, Mal would have kept Smith safely behind him. Instead, he presented her to him as his mate.

Apparently, Doyle was a real friend.

"Doyle, may I introduce my new bride, Smith."

Doyle bent low in a show of respect but did not touch. Smart.

"You are very beautiful, Smith. It is an honor to meet you."

"Smith, you may speak." Mal instructed.

Smith's back stiffened, although I doubted Mal saw

that from where he was standing. I, however, was at her back and very aware of the anger rising in her. "The honor is mine, Master Doyle."

"And this is my friend, Geros. We will be sharing our pleasure with Smith this evening. I assume everything has been prepared."

Doyle briefly greeted me, but I was of little interest to anyone, not with Smith standing here looking like a sensual goddess.

Mal led the way, Smith walking between us, to a room with a transparent front wall. Within the room was a padded table with obvious places for arms and legs, knees and elbows, that would place a submissive in a variety of sexual positions. Tools of pleasure--and pain-- hung from multiple hooks and lined small shelves along the back wall. Things I had seen before, many more that I had not.

Mal led us into the room and closed the door. The interior of the room was a shock, the walls, from this side, were black. Mal took Smith's hand and led her to the edge of the padded table. "Are you sure you are ready for this?"

She nibbled on her lower lip but held his gaze. "I'm sure. We have to make this look real if the other subs are going to talk to me." Her answer was quiet but determined.

"Agreed." He removed his shirt, leaving him wearing black boots and black pants, the tattoo on his wrist looked like a living, breathing thing as he moved under the lights. "What is your safe word?"

We had discussed this last night. All of it. The club. The sex. What would be expected and just how far she was willing to go. She had agreed to kissing, to some touching. She had agreed to allow us to give her at least one orgasm, and to receive a light punishment. Mal had asked her dozens of questions and she had answered him. Her forthright speech about what made her hot, what got her pussy wet and made her squirm? It had nearly killed me. Kayson had left the room halfway through the conversation. Only Mal had the discipline to sit, ask and listen. But then, this was his world, not mine.

I wanted to fuck her, fill her ass while Mal took her pussy and Kayson came in her mouth, but that was not to be. At least not today. Kayson was on watch from the roof of a nearby building making sure we weren't subject to any unwanted visitors or other surprises.

"Pumpkin."

"Pumpkin," Mal repeated. "I still do not understand this word."

"It's because I'm afraid I'll turn into one at midnight."

We both looked confused. She flushed and waved her hand to dismiss the topic. "Never mind. It's still pumpkin."

"Take your cover off, mate."

Smith's hands shook slightly as she removed her negligee. Her red lace panties were barely a string between the cheeks of her bottom. I could see moisture on the panties and her thighs. Her clit was a hard little nub pressed against the material.

I had to swallow at the sight.

Smith's hands went behind her back and she unhooked the bra, letting it fall away. Her breasts were full and golden, her dark nipples a hard contrast to their softness.

Mal stepped back. "Geros, touch her breasts."

I did as instructed, the soft skin heavy weights in my hands. Exquisite. I rolled her taut nipples with my thumbs. Smith moaned. "

"You like that, don't you?" Mal asked.

"Yes, Sir." She followed his lead and used the term 'Sir', as he'd instructed her last night.

"Does it make you hot and wet to have him touch you like this?"

"Yes."

He turned her and slapped her butt hard enough to leave a handprint—and she groaned. Her face flushed, her chest rising and falling quickly.

He smacked her other cheek, his hand leaving a second handprint. I watched her, saw her fists clench then relax. He slapped her ass several more times, alternating between cheeks, until her skin was pink and she was whimpering with each slap.

Mal turned her and she reached for him, tried to rub her breasts against his chest. Mal pulled away from her and stepped back. "I'm leaving for a minute. I'm going to go get some things I can use to play with you."

"Yes, Sir," she whispered.

He walked away. I watched her face, saw the eagerness in her eyes, the need driving her that she had, up until this moment, hidden from all three of us.

"I'll wait with you," I said as I pulled off my own shirt, my black pants and boots nearly identical to Mal's.

He returned and pushed her back against the wall, his massive body against her, his hand in her hair, turning her head to the side, baring her throat to me. I went to her, bending to kiss her exposed throat, claim it as mine, to follow the script we had worked out in advance.

She whimpered, her fists coming up to her mouth, her breath hitching as I kissed her then moved to her breasts, pinching her nipples, rolling them between my fingers, sucking on them until they peaked.

I moved to stand in front of her, taking her hands and placing them on my chest, stepping into her, kissing her lips. Mal stepped to the side, holding a leather flogger, three strands.

I kissed her until he tapped me on the shoulder, her taste an explosion on my senses. But she was holding back. This was still a farce. An imitation of real passion between mates.

He held out one hand and she placed her smaller hand in his, allowed him to lead her to the padded table.

I couldn't take my eyes off her. She was gorgeous.

He walked with her, positioning her where he wanted her to be. Then he placed his hand behind her neck and gently bent her over the end of the table. Once she was where he intended, he lifted her arms above her head and placed loops around her wrists which he secured to the table.

Smith tugged against them and quietly hissed over her shoulder. "Really? Is this necessary?"

"Yes. These Dom's know me and they know what I like. To leave you untethered would arouse suspicion. As you were told."

"I said I'd think about it."

"And so, have you? Thought about it?"

"Fine." She lifted up on her toes, her breath hitching as she looked over her shoulder at Mal. He handed me the flogger, then moved in front of her, his hand in her hair. Gently, her pulled her face toward his and stared into her eyes.

"Spread your feet apart," he growled, his voice strained. "Show Geros your hot pussy."

He watched her as she obeyed, her feet moving farther apart, her thighs open. Her pussy called to me, wet and glistening. Her tight little hole clenched and opened, just a bit, as if it were searching for something to fill it.

Me. Fuck. I wanted to fuck her there, in that tight little hole. And I wanted to do it while everyone on the other side of that wall watched me take what was mine.

Except she wasn't.

God this mission sucked.

"Geros, slide your fingers into her wet pussy."

I jolted as if I'd been in a trance and moved closer, stood between her spread thighs. Mal took the flogger from me so I was free to touch the woman who was not our mate.

Maybe this mission wasn't so bad after all.

Slowly, I slipped two fingers inside her heat. Her whimper was not of pain. I looked up to gauge her reaction. Her face was flushed, her eyes were dilated, her breathing heavy. The pulse at the base of her neck fluttered.

"Fuck her with your fingers while I give her what she needs."

I nodded. I wasn't going to call him Sir, but I was more than happy to be along for the ride. I slid my fingers in and out of her wet pussy, playing with her. Sometimes straight inside. Others at an angle. I tickled the inside of her pussy walls and ran my fingertips around the opening like tracing the rim off a drinking glass.

Mal watched for long minutes until she lifted her hips, trying to take more of me, a light sheen of sweat on her back making her shimmer.

He smacked her bottom with the flogger.

"Ouch!" She jolted at the contact.

"What is your safe word?"

"Pumpkin."

"Do you wish to use it? Do you want me to stop?" Mal asked.

The silence seemed to stretch to eternity, but I knew it was less than a minute.

"No, Sir."

My cock was so engorged I felt as if the skin would burst at any moment. I was in physical pain. I knew Mal could be no different, not with the scent of her wet pussy filling the small room.

He ran the flogger lightly against her bottom, and she flinched. He struck her again, the leather strands slapping against her cheeks leaving a red mark, the sting of it making her cry out. He flogged her again, the strands hitting hard, a louder, more intense slap that made her moan and her pussy clench. He used the flogger on her back. Her side. He struck the sides of her breasts as I fucked her with my fingers. As her pussy became wetter. More swollen.

He smacked her bottom with the flogger again and she wiggled, pushing back onto my fingers, forcing me to go deeper. I added a third finger. She groaned. He used the flogger on her thigh. Her body went stiff.

"Do you like that?" He checked in with her again.

"Yes, Sir."

He looked to me and I nodded. Each time the flogger made contact with her skin her pussy clamped down on my fingers.

Mal struck her again and again, until her ass was a deep red.

He walked away to place the flogger back on one of the shelves. She protested.

"No. Don't stop."

"Geros, kiss her. Shut her up."

I changed position, walking around the table until I was close enough to bend down and take her lips. But first I lifted my hand and slid my fingers into my mouth, tasting her sweet essence. Breathing her in.

She watched me as if she couldn't look away. Our gazes locked, the intimacy of the moment shocking. Her gaze was focused, intense, locked on me as the taste of her wet heat exploded on my tongue and branded itself into my being.

I lowered my head and kissed her. The angle was awkward but her wrists were bound. I lifted her shoulders and tilted her body toward mine, just enough to gain full access to her mouth. I needed to taste her.

I expected the same kiss she'd given me before. Controlled. Restrained. She was neither. She was ravenous, kissing me like she'd never get enough, like I was her air and her heart needed me to keep beating.

One moment I was a sentient being and the next I was an animal who needed nothing more than to claim my mate. I knew the blackness of the walls was an illusion. I knew that at this moment there were probably dozens of eyes witnessing our actions, watching this beautiful female kiss me. Choose me. Give herself to me.

I tore my lips from hers but she nibbled along the corners of my mouth. My jaw. "I know what you are, Geros. Sector One. I know what you want."

By the gods. "And what is that?"

"To fuck me in my ass while all those people outside watch you do it."

Fuck. Fuck. Fuck. "Why are you saying this to me? We had a plan." I tried to keep my voice low as I pressed my lips to her ear, but Mal heard the conversation anyway.

"Is that what you want, mate?" He spoke loudly, clearly. I assumed so those outside the walls might hear his words.

Smith was still bent over the table, her feet apart, her ass hanging off the end in blatant invitation. "Yes. That is what I want, Sir." She looked up at Mal. "I want him in my ass and I want you in my mouth."

I thought Mal's head might explode when she licked her lips. Mine would have. Instead he met her gaze with a calm I envied.

"No."

Her gasp expressed both her shock and mine. Mal had placed the flogger to the side and held a smaller object. I looked closely and saw a slim dildo with an attachment that would fit over her clit, sucking and vibrating.

Was he going to put that in her pussy? Was this happening? Did she mean what she was saying? She *wanted* me to take her? Fill her?

I felt the pre-cum leak from the end of my cock. I was fucking shaking. This was insanity.

"Are you sure about this?" I looked down into Smith's eyes. "I am a male with healthy appetites. I will not turn down what you freely offer."

She closed her eyes as if she couldn't look at me and admit the truth. "Do it. I want you to do it."

I nodded and walked to the end of the table, Smith's red bottom and glistening pussy on display. Mal joined me. I watched, mesmerized, as Mal slowly moved the thin line of red fabric even farther to the side and slipped the dildo into Smith's pussy. She moaned and widened her legs. Mal obliged and pushed it a bit deeper. He also placed a small, smooth object into her tight hole. I knew that tablet would dissolve, create a smooth, wet slide inside her body for my cock.

"More." Her forehead was pressed to the table, her knuckles white where she held on to its edges.

"No. You will take all of Geros. That will be enough." He ran his hand along her thigh, up over the curve of her ass, her back, and tangled his fingers in her hair. He turned her head gently, angling her face so she would be looking at him. "What do you call me, mate?"

"Sir. More, Sir."

Mal turned his head and nodded to me. "I have placed sufficient lubrication. She should be ready for you." He looked back down at Smith even as he spoke to me. "And do not be gentle."

I would have protested but Smith moaned. Her pussy spasmed, nearly dislodging the dildo. I pushed the device back into place and freed my cock from my pants. I wanted this. I wanted *her*.

I wanted my cock buried deep. I wanted everyone on the other side of these glass walls to know she had chosen me, given me this gift. I wanted to fuck her so thoroughly that she would never want to be with another male.

This was not part of the plan. Not the fucking plan...

I grabbed her hip, my hand nearly wrapping around it, and used my free hand to place my cock at her tight little hole. I moved slowly, pushed the bulbous head of my cock into her ass.

She had been holding her breath. As I moved into her, she exhaled slowly, sweetly. I started to push forward until I encountered resistance. Smith held perfectly still, her breathing shallow and quick. I pressed forward, gradually stretching her, until the head of my cock popped inside.

I wanted to slam my hips forward, to ram my cock all the way into her, to brand her as mine, but I knew it would hurt her. I pulled back slightly, then pushed forward gently.

She cried out, her muscles contracting around me like a vise. I paused, not certain, until I felt the echoes of the vibrations coming from the device Mal had attached to her clit. He had her head in a firm grasp, his gaze locked with hers so there was nowhere for her to look but at him.

"Harder, Geros. Our little mate likes a touch of pain with her pleasure."

My balls drew up tight and I held back my orgasm by sheer force of will. I was not ready for this to end.

I moved in and out of her, the space occupied by the dildo making her ass that much tighter, that much sweeter. This was how it would feel with Mal fucking her pussy. We would both be filling her, pleasuring her. Claiming her.

But this wasn't a true claiming. That would require all three of us to take her together. And her consent. Her vow to be ours, to stay with us as our mate. A family.

She was not our bride. Not ours.

Not mine.

With my cock balls deep inside her, I couldn't allow myself to think about that.

I began slowly, but when she squirmed and pushed back against me, I thrust forward. Hard.

"That's it, Geros. That's how she likes it." Mal's voice was a deep rumble.

Fuck me. I wasn't going to last.

I pumped in and out of her ass, driven on by her mewling sounds of pleasure. Finally, when I could take no more, Mal bent down and kissed Smith on the cheek. "Come now, Smith. Come hard. Give Geros everything."

As if he'd flipped a switch, Smith's entire body went stiff, arching up off the table. The pulsing of her pussy muscles broke the last bit of my control and my seed pumped into her as I shuddered.

When I was calm, I pulled out slowly before leaning over to kiss the curve of her spine. "Thank you, Smith."

She rolled as far onto her side as the restraints would allow. She looked down at me, her eyes glazed, unfocused. We had done that to her. Me and Mal. I could only imagine what it would be like if Kayson joined us as well.

Mal came to her hip, reached around her thigh and slipped the dildo from pussy. She jumped when he detached the vibration device from her clit.

"So sensitive, mate." He moved to the shelves and tossed a towel at me. "Clean yourself up. I'll take care of her. Then we'll go have a drink and she can relax with the other submissives."

That had been the plan all along. Act the part of the besotted, devoted mates. Give her an orgasm and then send her on her way to infiltrate and gossip and do what she'd come here to do—make people tell her their secrets, hunt assassins and killers.

Nothing had gone according to plan so far. Nothing. I had fucked her. My Seed Power was already melting into her system, bonding her to me and me to her. The languid look in her eyes was not all from her orgasm. My seed provided her that pleasure, that warmth and comfort, and desire for more. Once her body had fully processed my gift, her scent would drive me mad with need. The smell of her pussy would call to me with a power that was nearly impossible to resist.

Viken mates did not cheat, not because there was a lack of willing partners, but because nothing else could compare to the bond with a mate.

I would never want another female the way I wanted her. Question was, what the fuck was I going to do about it?

 *mith*

I WALKED TOWARD THE SUBMISSIVES' lounge, my body still tingling. Doms weren't allowed in there. When Mal first told me that, I'd considered it only as a strategic advantage. Now I needed the personal space to get away from them.

From myself.

What the hell had I just done?

I'd begged a complete stranger to fuck me in the ass. That's what I'd done. I'd stared into Mal's eyes as it happened, watching him as he analyzed every whimper, every expression on my face. He somehow knew what I wanted. I didn't have to tell him I liked pain. That'd I'd always liked pain. Even when I was a child, I would seek out other kids and play foolish games. Rub our skin off with an eraser. Slap one another's hands. Hold our palms over a candle and see how long we could take the pain as our skin burned.

I always won. And I always wanted to play.

I'd grown up, but I'd never grown out of it. I'd done some research once. The psychiatrists called it a craving for *extreme sensation.* That flogger landing on my ass was extreme, all right. And I'd almost had an orgasm from an alien I barely knew basically whipping me.

No. Not whipping. I'd heard someone here, though, crying through an old school whipping. I wondered what that would feel li—

No. Shut up. Shut the hell up, Carmen.

I'd always been different. I knew something was wrong with me. My mother swore I was possessed by a demon and stopped taking me to the doctor after some of my more foolish, painful stunts. But I'd never felt evil. As a girl I'd been shamed and convinced I wasn't normal. As a woman, I'd buried my needs under rules and regulations and the expectations of others.

I couldn't believe how much of myself I gave away so quickly.

"Welcome, little one." The gigantic Dom watching the door held it open for me. His eyes were a grayish color, but kind. Like a big teddy bear's would be. He felt safe.

"Thank you, Sir." I almost wrapped my arms around him and cried my eyes out. But that wasn't professional, was it? Was it?!

And getting fucked in the ass with a bunch of strangers watching IS professional?

I told that annoying little wench in my head to shut up and kept going. I couldn't undo what I'd just done.

Still, I wondered, had that big teddy bear ever flogged a grown woman?

Why was I even wondering about this?

Was I going crazy? Why didn't I feel guilty? Maybe I did. If I didn't, I wouldn't be having this stupid conversation with myself.

Shit. I was supposed to be on mission and all I could think about was sex.

The door closed softly behind me. I took a deep breath and tried to steady my nerves. But how was I supposed to concentrate now? I could feel the heatwaves still rising off my skin. Worse, this Seed Power thing was for *real.*

Geros had come inside me. I'd known the instant his semen made contact with my flesh. Warmth. Contentment. I'd never felt anything like it. Instant...bliss. The spreading tingles had caused little aftershock orgasms to flood my pussy for what felt like forever. Mal had been cleaning me up—another embarrassing first—and I'd still been having miniature orgasms.

Even more humiliating? The whole time, Mal had barely touched me. He'd done exactly what we'd scripted out ahead of time. But when I went off the rails, he pushed me over the edge, but refused to come with us.

Geros? He'd been all in. Of course he had been. I'd

offered him what every man wanted, right? But I'd offered Mal the same. He'd said no so fast I didn't have time to process before Geros was taking my ass. After his big cock pushed deep, there hadn't been much thinking going on other than *more*.

Had I made a mistake? A huge, terrible, stupid mistake?

"Come on in. You're new. I saw you come in with Master Mal." A much older woman gently touched my elbow and I allowed her to steer me to an empty space on one of the plush sofas.

"Thank you."

She chuckled, left for a moment and returned with a tall glass full of what looked like water. Suddenly, I was nearly dead from thirst. I drank it all and handed the glass back to her with a sheepish smile. "Thanks."

"Of course." She left and returned moments later, this time to settle next to me on the sofa. "Are you alright? Do you need anything else? Anything at all? Master Mal has a reputation for being," she paused. "Intense."

I burst into laughter and a few more ladies gathered around us. The room was dimly lit, with soft pink and purple hues illuminating the space. At least a dozen women and half as many men, all dressed in various forms of lingerie or—other revealing clothing—lounged around the room. Some were sitting on plush velvet couches, while others sprawled out on oversized plump chairs designed to easily hold at least two people. They were all eating snacks and sipping on glasses of various colored drinks. Their laughter and chatter filled the air. The atmosphere was relaxed and carefree, a stark contrast to my current state of mind.

But a perfect place to share secrets.

I scanned the room, taking in the diverse group of subs. One woman, with long blonde hair and a red lace teddy, sat perched on the arm of a couch, a glass of dark red wine in her hand. She was laughing and chatting animatedly with the other women, her face alight with joy. Another, with short black hair and a black corset, lounged on a rug that looked thick enough to sleep on. She sat with her legs out in front of her, ankles crossed. Her shoes glittered like diamonds, her legs crossed at the ankle. She was more reserved, her eyes scanning the room as if taking in everything that was happening around her.

The women around me all leaned in, their eyes sparkling with curiosity.

"So? Master Mal? How was it?" one of the blonde women asked, her lips curved into a knowing grin. "He's been gone forever." She made it sound like a complaint, as if she had been personally waiting for him to come back.

Jealousy roared inside me like the monster it was at the thought of him touching her. Flogging her. Telling someone how to bring her pleasure. I had to take a deep, slow breath to keep myself from saying something really, really stupid. Mal wasn't mine.

I was never this out of control. What. The. Fuck? Had

Geros's Seed Power really messed with my head that much?

It was the orgasms, dummy. The talking wench was back.

My face instantly became as hot as the fire still burning my bottom. "It was... intense." There was no other word to describe the experience. At least none that I would share here. I heard the shake in my voice and clasped my hands. They were clammy. My ass was on fire and my hands were freezing.

Great. I really was losing it.

"Intense is one way to put it," the black-haired woman said with a laugh. "But from the looks of it, I'd say it was pretty amazing." Her tone was soft and understanding, as if she could sense the turmoil I was going through. "My master wanted to watch. I hope that's all right."

"Of course." What else was I going to say. I'd known what was going down. I just hadn't realized how much it would affect my emotional stability. I felt like I'd had my legs swept out from under me and I couldn't quite get my feet back on the ground.

"We watched, too. It was amazing," another said, her voice barely above a whisper.

The women all cooed and oohed, their attention fully me.

"So, how did you manage to steal the club's most eligible male? Every sub in here was after him at one time or another. Except me." The older woman who'd first helped me chuckled. "I've been with my master for twenty years. He knows what I like. No sense looking for a new one."

The group giggled in agreement. I hesitated, not sure exactly what would be the most effective way to earn trust with this group of strangers. But they were all looking at me expectantly, their eyes filled with excitement. I took a deep breath before answering. "He's my new mate. I just met him yesterday."

"You're an Interstellar Bride?"

"Yes. From Earth." I answered the second question before anyone could ask.

"Like the queen. That Earth?"

"Yes."

Squeals of delight filled our corner of the room and more people began to migrate toward the commotion. Which was exactly what I thought I wanted, before I didn't *know* what I wanted.

"Did you know her? On Earth?" Someone asked. I couldn't make out which woman had spoken.

I smiled. "No. Earth's a pretty big place. I never met her."

"Oh, I want to meet her."

"I just want to fuck those three kings of hers. Can you imagine?" Another voice filled the room, this one masculine.

"You already took away Master Niven. Leave some for the rest of us!" The woman next to me wagged a finger at the man. The room burst into appreciative giggles and sounds of agreement.

"Who's Master Niven?" I asked.

"He's that big hunk guarding the door," his sub answered.

"Oh." Teddy bear man? And yes, he'd had a whip in his hands last I saw him.

"I see that look in your eyes." The man looked at me, but he was smiling. "He's mine and I'm not letting him go."

"I have my hands full. Trust me."

"She came in with Master Mal," someone explained.

"Oooh. Do tell." The woman on my right leaned in so close her body heat irritated the flog marks on my shoulders.

I leaned in closer, until we touched. A sliver of pain sliced down my back and I shuddered with pleasure.

"You're like me. I can see it in your eyes. And on your back." The young man, Nevin's sub, had walked closer. His words weren't unkind, more one friend whispering secrets to another. I could see him clearly now. He was attractive, muscled—as all these Viken males seemed to be. He was younger than me, but not by much. He'd been the one begging to be taken when I'd first come in with Mal and Geros. I'd tried not to stare, but I'd never seen anything like their scene before. And I was guilty of imagining a bunch of things I shouldn't be thinking about. But not with his big teddy bear man. With mine.

No. Not mine. Not. Mine.

He turned around in a slow swirl and showed me his bare back. A crisscross of red, angry marks covered him.

Upon closer inspection, he looked as flushed and pink skinned as I felt. Everywhere. Was that what I looked like right now? My back and my bottom were on fire. I'd never felt so completely satisfied in my life.

From the dreamy look in the other subs eyes, none of the submissive females in this room would stand a chance at stealing his teddy bear anyway.

I stayed and chatted with the subs for over an hour, discreetly asking questions. Most of the subs in the room were influential, powerful people in the outside world. They were either in a power position themselves, or their significant others were important people in the city, some of them with connections to law enforcement or politicians, others with ties to the criminal underworld.

This was the kind of room where deals were made. Secrets shared. I had no doubt that wherever Geros and Mal were right now, they were probably having a similar experience. But then again, perhaps not.

Once they knew I was new to their world, they all felt an obsessive need to educate me on the way things worked on Viken. Who was who. Where the best shops were. The best entertainment. Gossip about Viken's royal family—which I listened to with a bit of a laugh because half of what they said was only marginally accurate and the rest was rubbish. But that was fame, apparently on any planet.

The conversation around me was lively, with the women discussing everything from sexual positions to politics. But then, one of them made a comment about a recent assassination attempt on the princess of their planet. Every instinct I had went on high alert.

"Can you believe it? Someone actually tried to kill the princess," she said, her voice filled with shock and disbelief.

The other women around the table were similarly unhappy, some enraged. Murmurs of disbelief and condemnation filled the room as various conspiracy theories were offered and dismissed. But there was one woman who didn't react as she should have, not if she had any care or concern for the royal family. Instead, she was quiet, her expression unreadable, and she didn't seem to be as interested in the topic as the others.

I watched her closely, my suspicions growing. She was difficult to study. She kept to the edges of the group, rarely adding to the conversation. She wore a very revealing negligee, as the rest of the females did, but there was a distinct area on the side of each thigh where the material was thick and opaque. And big enough to hide a weapon.

One by one the subs began to leave, looking for their partners, ready to go home. I leaned close to the older woman who'd stayed by my side and pointed out the quiet one. "Who is that? She's so quiet."

"Oh, she's harmless. She's Master Gee's sub. Morna. He's out of town a lot. She comes down here because she's lonely."

"Doesn't she have neighbors or friends she can talk to?" It seemed very odd to me that she would come all the way down to the club, dressed like *that,* when a call to a friend or a walk at the park—they did have parks here, right?—would serve her better.

"Oh, no. She lives upstairs. And her master doesn't allow her to go out alone. He has to be with her. Very unhealthy, that relationship. But you didn't hear that from me. No one cares about the opinion of an old woman."

I cared. I cared a lot. "Thank you for taking me under your wing tonight. I was a little out of it when I came in here."

She smiled at me, the kind of smile that makes you want to throw your arms around a dear friend and hold on. "It's always like that, dear. When they break down one of your walls. It takes a while to recover."

Break down one of my walls?

She patted me on the hand and left to find her mate. I finished my—by now—third glass of water and took the opportunity to approach the Morna, the quiet one who lived upstairs in an unhealthy relationship with a Dom who sounded like an asshole. But that was just me making assumptions.

"Excuse. Sorry. I just—I know I look a mess and I was wondering if there was a place I could try to at least do something with my hair?"

She nodded, took one last look around the room as if reluctant to leave. "Come on. I'll show you. It's on the way upstairs."

"What's upstairs?" I already knew, but I wanted to know if she would tell me the truth.

"Our apartment. There are six Doms who have suites on the upper floors. I live on the third floor with Master Gee."

"Oh, that's wonderful. Congratulations. Have you been living with him a long time?"

She looked at me like I had a screw loose. Which I felt like I probably did.

"Three years, which is two years too long."

"I'm confused. Why don't you move out?"

"We love who we love. Sometimes that's a good thing. Sometimes it's not." I had followed her out a side door of the lounge, through a short hallway lined with soft, padded carpet of some kind, to a white door. She pointed to the door. "Here we are. You can freshen up in here. We have everything you could possibly need."

"Thanks. I'm Smith."

"I know." She smiled, a small, pathetic, sad smile and turned to walk up a set of stairs. "Maybe I'll see you next time."

She didn't wait for me to respond, just walked up the stairs, turned on a landing and disappeared. I waited about thirty seconds. Then I followed her.

I was careful to keep my distance, I didn't want to draw her attention. And I didn't want to have to come up with a bullshit lie about why I was sneaking after her on the stairs.

My heart raced as I followed Morna, my mind racing with possibilities. Was this woman somehow connected to the assassination attempt? Was she involved in some way? Or was it her Dom, Master Gee. Mal had not mentioned that name, but I tucked it away to ask about later.

Morna finally came to a stop in front of a door that was guarded by a man with a rough, menacing look. He was even bigger than the teddy bear man downstairs. I watched as she knocked on the door, and a moment later, it was opened.

A male voice came from inside. "What are you doing here? He told you where to sleep, Morna. He will punish you."

"I need to speak with him." Morna's voice was low and urgent. "It's important."

The voice shifted to a chuckle. "You do like the whip, don't you?"

"Someone asked me about the princess. He needs to know."

"I will convey your message."

"No!" The door slammed in her face.

I watched Morna argue with the guard. He did not raise his voice or speak unkindly, but he also would not allow her to pass. Morna stood there for a moment as if trying to gather her thoughts. Then she turned on her heel and disappeared down a hallway I could not see from this vantage point.

"You there. Female. What are you doing here?" The

guard's deep voice bellowed down the hall. I'd had *maybe* one eye and a whisp of hair in view.

He wasn't just big, he was sharp.

I knew I needed to report this to the guys. I had to get out of here. Only one thing left to do--bluff.

Putting on a mask of innocent bafflement, I walked straight up to the guard and looked at the floor, everything in my posture non-threatening. Submissive. As if the almost nothing of a sheer, red nighty, g-string panties and an almost nothing push-up bra weren't enough to clue him in to my status in the club. "I'm so sorry, Sir. It's my first time here. But I took a wrong turn. I was too afraid to ask for help. I just kept going and now I don't know where I am."

"Do not worry." His voice was kind, even if his body was frightening. "I cannot leave my post, but I will summon someone from within to escort you back to your master."

"My mate." The words tumbled out of me and I hoped that somehow a mate would offer even more protection in this place than a master would. It appeared I was correct.

"One moment, my lady. Please, come in. I will call a replacement and walk you back myself."

"Thank you, Sir." I still had not looked him in the eye. I did, however, get a rather long look at the growing bulge in his pants.

Were all Viken hung like horses? Good god.

"My pleasure, my lady." The guard opened the door

and led the way inside.

I shouldn't go in alone. I knew that. But this wasn't my first assignment. However, it was the first time I'd walked into an unknown space without my gun. And not just any unknown space. Oh, no. This one had to be on another freaking planet in a sex club. Shit, my mother would be rolling over in her grave. She'd thought running drugs for a cartel had been dangerous. At least when I did that, I'd worn clothes.

The guard was tall and muscular—seemed they were all built big on Viken—but much older than Mal, Geros and Kayson. Probably twenty years older, if I had to guess. The lines of scars on his forearms and neck made me think he'd been a soldier at some point.

"Stay here, my lady, while I inform the others."

"Of course, Sir." The last word was like acid in my mouth. Every time I had to say it to this Viken guard it got worse. It was nothing like saying it to Mal. No, calling Mal Sir made me want to purr like a kitten, crawl into his lap and let him take care of me. Or fuck me. Or order someone else to do it. Whatever he wanted.

Just like Geros. He'd been so desperate to fuck me I'd feared he was going to have a stroke. Every muscle in his body had been tense, his blood vessels bulging from his temple and neck. I'd given him a gift and that made me really, really happy. Which was freaking weird, but when was the last time anyone other than my boss had asked me for anything.

Too damn long. Years. Maybe a decade or more.

I really was losing it, feeling sorry for myself and my pathetic, lonely life when I should be looking for clues.

The place felt empty. Not like no one occupied the space, but as if even the walls were afraid to make a sound. I crept quietly down the hallway, my heart pounding in my chest. The big guard's footsteps were loud. Heavy. I would hear him before I would see him. I knew I had to be careful – if I was caught snooping around the apartment, I'd be in a lot of trouble. Maybe. Depended how easy the big guard was to dupe.

I passed by a few closed doors, eyes scanning for any signs of movement. But so far, everything was quiet. I took a deep breath and kept moving forward, my hand on the entrance panel to what looked like a study on Earth. Or a personal library.

Thankfully, the door made almost no sound as it slid open. I peered inside. The room was dimly lit, I could make out a few pieces of furniture. I crept inside, my eyes looking for any clues. I spotted a photograph on the mantelpiece and picked it up, studying it closely.

Just as I was about to put the photograph back, I heard a noise behind me. I spun around, my heart racing. But it was just a creature of some kind, agile like cat, and about the same size. Some kind of pet sauntered into the room. I sighed in relief, but my heart was still pounding. The creature eyed me with curiosity and stayed close. Which was a good thing. If I was caught back here, I could blame it on the creature somehow. Say I heard it crying?

Did these things make noise? Damn. I'd have to say I just saw it running or something.

I continued to search, looking for anything that might link the owner to the VSS or the princess. I rifled through drawers and opened closets but found nothing. Just as I was about to give up, I spotted a small box tucked away near the very back of a shelf inside a small, tucked away cabinet in the corner of the room.

I opened it. Inside was something that looked eerily like a tablet back home. Except this one seemed to be motion activated because it turned on, its screen bright and the image clear.

Oh, god.

I looked at the top several images, flipping between them quickly with a swipe of my finger. There were more, but I didn't dare take the time to look through all of them. There were at least fifty images here. The stakes had just gone up.

If they found me with this, they'd kill me.

My heart skipped a beat as I replaced the device, closed the box and pushed it back into the far corner of the cabinet. Those images were of the queen and a little girl who had to be her daughter, same red hair, same smile. It was clear that whoever had taken the first picture knew the queen personally, as she was staring directly into the camera and her smile was genuine, not forced.

Hands shaking, I quickly put everything back exactly as I had found it. There were more photos of the queen and her daughter on that device, obviously taken some time in the past. But the one that made my blood run cold was of that same little girl, the princess, in some kind of transparent, coffin-looking thing, just like Snow White in the forest. That had to be a ReGen pod. I'd never seen one, so I couldn't' be sure. However, these images gave irrefutable proof that there was indeed a traitor *inside* the palace. Not just any traitor, but someone the queen trusted.

I couldn't leave with the device. I nowhere to hide it. Literally. I was basically naked. Could I sneak one past the guard? Not a good idea. The tablet was not small, the device having laid across both of my palms. Too large to hide in my hand. I didn't have shoes, the subs here didn't wear them inside. Mine were with Mal. Somewhere.

I couldn't swallow it and I couldn't shove it up my hoo-ha, so I had to leave it here. They would just have to believe me when I told them what I'd seen.

Time to get out of here.

I made my way to the door.

I stepped into the corridor, but the stubborn pet-thing refused to leave the room.

Damn it. I didn't have time to deal with a stubborn, alien cat cousin. They'd just have to wonder how the stupid creature ended up in that room.

Just as the door slid closed, I heard heavy footsteps coming at a rapid pace. I froze just long enough to make sure I knew what direction they were coming from. I ran on silent feet back to the room where the guard had left me.

A door opened behind me, but I didn't dare look back. I kept moving forward, toward a window that over-looked the city. If the guard noticed my movement, I could only hope he would assume I had been nervous. Pacing.

I needed to leave. Now. Now. Right now. I controlled the urge to run, as I had hundreds of times before, the calm on my face the opposite of the turmoil in my mind. I controlled my breathing and turned when the sound of the guard's footsteps were directly behind me.

"I apologize for the delay. I can take you back to the salon now, my lady."

"Thank you, Sir. I am afraid I would get lost again on my own." I kept my gaze demurely on my hands where they were clasped in front of me. I made sure my chest was on full frontal display.

"Of course, little one. Follow me." His gaze drifted exactly where I wanted it to, which meant he didn't look too closely at my face or notice that I was a bit out of breath from the mad dash back here.

Little one? Of course he would call me that. I'd acted the part of a docile lamb and called him 'Sir' when he wasn't my master, my lover, my *anything*.

Score one for the helpless damsel in distress routine. It had never worked for me before. But then, I'd never been dressed like a horny man's half-naked fantasy before, either.

The image of the little princess laying in a coma made the blood in my legs turn to ice-cold sludge. I had to get back to Mal and Geros or no one would know what I'd found.

I followed the guard like a lost puppy despite the fact that I knew exactly where I was in the building. My sense of direction had always been excellent. A few twisty hallways were nothing to the underground tunnels I'd crawled through on the border.

I really hoped this guy would taking me where he was supposed to. I didn't want to fight him. My only chance would be to take him out immediately. Not good odds. He was big, not an ounce of fat on him. No need to tempt fate unless absolutely necessary. In all honesty, and I generally tried to be honest, at least with myself, I didn't think I could take him. Some men, yes. Not this one. Every move screamed fighter. Soldier. Killer.

Being nearly naked didn't help my confidence, either.

He took a strange turn.

Shit.

I mentally planned my attack. Take out the knees, go for the throat. If that failed, I'd have to try and crush his skull with bare feet. It didn't take as much force as one would think. But...gross.

He took two more steps. I lagged, preparing for my speed run at his knees.

Stop.

I recognized the decorations on the walls, could hear the sounds of the club once more.

The guard opened a concealed door for me, held it for me just as the big teddy bear man had.

He smiled. "Be careful, little one."

"Thank you, Sir." I walked away from him as quickly as I could without running. He would probably assume I was scared of the big, bad man. Really, that was true. More that his boss might order him to kill me before I could leave the building and tell anyone else what I had seen.

I glanced over my shoulder to make sure the door had closed behind me. Yes. Good. Unfortunately, I looked around, really looked. This was not where I had been before. This the main room we had passed when first entering the club. The one they'd walked by and ignored. The room with a lot more people. A lot more.

This was the room where big teddy bear man had ignored his subs pleas and turned his back into a mish-mash of hot, red welts. Like mine.

The music was loud. People were writhing and kissing, nearly fucking on the dance floor. I couldn't look away. I didn't want to. Instead, my gaze traveled from one erotic experience to the next, the images I'd found of the queen and princess fading to the background as I watched these Viken people embrace their bodies and their pleasures without holding back. Geros's Seed Power flared again, sending heat to my core, my breasts.

God how I envied them. Every single one.

None of them had been raised Catholic. That was for damn sure.

There was nothing to do but wait for Mal and Geros to find me. Well, nothing important enough to drag me away from *this*.

Within five minutes I'd been asked to give one man a blow job while his gay lover watched, invited to join a group of seven very enthusiastic--and very public--lovers switching partners and laughing as they sipped wine and fucked. I made my way close to what I knew was the entrance and came upon a space with one man and two women tied to poles, their wrists bound, their naked backs exposed for their masters' whims. One was being tickled with a feather. Another flogged--as I had been. Damn it all, my pussy got wet all over again watching them.

The need for a bite of pain with my pleasure had scared off more than one potential boyfriend. So I'd learned to bury it, only indulge when I was alone. Which sucked, but I'd never been able to trust anyone enough to show them my darkness. My need. I'd been taught my whole life that it was wrong. But here? Now? No one passed judgment. Sex was sex. Pleasure was pleasure. No one seemed to care about anything but enjoying them-selves. Not like the human men who found me odd, or dangerous. Who turned away.

Mal didn't turn away. The thought rushed into my head like an unwanted bomb exploding. No, he'd somehow known what to do to make my body sing.

Well, he had spent over an hour questioning me about every lover I'd ever had. What I'd tried and what I'd not. How he'd known to order Geros to be a bit rough, I had no idea. I had been very careful to keep my darker urges out of that conversation

So he'd had a lucky guess. Or perhaps that was just the way *he* was, what *he* liked.

I would tell him nothing. Moderate myself. Stay in control. I wasn't keeping them. I wasn't staying on this planet. They weren't mine. Acting otherwise was a recipe for disaster.

Speaking of my colleagues slash sex partners, where were they? Why was it taking them so long to find me?

7

Mal

The music was loud and the crowd was thick as Geros and I pushed our way through the club. We were both frantically searching for Smith, who had entered the Subs' lounge and never came back out. Geros did little to hide his frustration, but I was watched here. If I acted like a lovesick fool or showed any fear, it would be noted, gossiped about and possibly put Smith in danger.

That was unacceptable.

"I knew this was a bad idea. We never should have let her go in there alone."

"It's their safe space, Geros. Doms are not allowed for a reason." Mostly because not one of us could tolerate the idea of another Dom having unsupervised access to our subs. But we told ourselves the lie and the subs did seem to enjoy relaxing in one another's company.

As we made our way through the sea of people, the mix of perfumes, colognes and sex grew thick and heavy. The overpowering scent revolting after being in a room with Smith and her sweet, wet pussy.

I knew Smith was a professional. On Earth. But this was Viken. This was not her world. This club? Nothing she'd spoken of when I interviewed her even came close. She'd been locked inside her body, holding on tight. I'd cracked her shell tonight. Created an open wound that would need tending. That hadn't been my intention, but I'd looked into her eyes and instinct had taken over.

I'd been a fucking selfish idiot. I'd never done this before, broken a sub and then not been there to hold her, to put her back together again. Stronger. Wiser. More comfortable with herself and her needs.

I'd cracked Smith open and sent her out to hunt for assassins and traitors. If she was hurt because of me, I would never forgive myself.

And something *had* happened to her. I couldn't shake the feeling that something was wrong. She'd been gone too long. I needed to find her. I needed to know she was unharmed.

Geros was in a similarly remorseful state, his mind consumed with worry as he scanned the faces in the crowd. "I never should have accepted her offer. She wasn't in her right mind."

"She was."

"No, Mal, she wasn't. I listened to your conversation with her. She's never been to a place like this. She's never been flogged or hurt in any way. What the fuck was I thinking? I didn't hold back. She wasn't prepared properly. I hurt her."

I could barely hear him over the music. We moved across the dance floor toward the entrance, the heat and sweat of the dancing people around us pressing in on me.

This was why I'd stopped coming here. These people all needed something. Every single one of them. For some it was simple. A kind word. Someone to hold them. For others it was not so simple. Pain. Pleasure. Service. Mastery. Some loved nothing but pain. Others loved nothing more than causing it.

I was none of these things. These people were hurting, and it was in my nature to try to give others what they needed. No matter the cost to myself. So I'd left this life behind. There were too many broken hearts. Too many shattered souls I could not heal. I'd felt like a failure even as, more and more, they clamored for my attention.

This place had nearly sucked the life out of me. Killed me dead. That's when Geros and Kayson had found me, convinced me to join the war, the Coalition Fleet. Hurting things, killing things, had sounded like a good outlet for my pent-up pain.

Even that had failed me. I'd killed our enemies, yet every time I still saw the Prillon warrior or Viken fighter beneath the implants, behind their blank stares. Killing them had been a mercy, an act of service, and even then, I could not escape giving away pieces of myself.

"I can't shake the feeling that something is wrong."
Geros' thought mirrored my own. Not comforting.

I had been searching for what felt like hours and had
yet to find any sign of her. The club would become
increasingly dangerous for Smith as the night went on.

There was only one more place to look. Surely, she
would not—

And yet, she was. I relaxed for the first time in hours
and grabbed Geros by the arm. When he turned, I
pointed to a place beyond a few gyrating bodies on the
dance floor. She was standing alone, her arms crossed
tightly, her eyes overly bright. I moved in to stand behind
her and frowned at the condition she'd allowed herself to
be in. She was freezing cold, her flesh pebbled and cool
to the touch. She didn't respond to my nudge of her
shoulder. The dancers must have bumped into her
repeatedly for her to ignore the contact.

Or she was so engrossed in the flogging scene playing
out before her that she could not look away.

I wanted to watch her a bit longer, determine if the
glazed look in her eyes was need or fear. If she was para-
lyzed with disbelief, a need to watch the grotesque, or
envy for the sub who's master flogged her as she
screamed. I knew the sub well, had been on the other
side of the flogger more than once. She was one who
needed someone to help her release her rage, her pent-
up frustration. Her fear and tension. She could not do it
alone. She needed someone to force her to release the
stronger emotions.

Smith barely moved, hardly blinked.

Geros broke the spell. "Are you alright?"

She turned to face us, moving slowly, the empty space in her mind filling with thoughts once again. "I'm fine." She pasted on a very bright, completely dishonest smile. Her voice was trembling. "Shall we go?"

Geros led the way to the entrance. I made them wait as I retrieved Smith's cloak. The night air was cool and she was not wearing enough to keep her warm.

I refused to think about the fact that leaving Club Trinity would allow anyone outside of the club to see her body, my marks on her back, and it filled me with protective rage. Those things were personal. Private.

Mine.

We rode the short distance to our rented apartment in silence, Kayson driving our rented EV. Smith spent the entire ride staring out the window. Geros and I spent the time watching her.

We had agreed in advance to discuss nothing of importance until we were safely inside the walls of our residence. We'd thoroughly checked the rooms for any type of technology that could monitor us or overhear our conversations. We'd found the usual, standard tech meant to be used by law enforcement or in medical emergencies.

We'd disabled those as well.

The moment the door closed behind the four of us, Kayson was glaring. "What the fuck happened tonight? You were supposed to be out of there an hour ago."

Smith smiled. "What happened tonight, gentlemen, was victory. Third floor. Someone called Master Gee. There is a tablet in his office with dozens of pictures of the queen and Allayna. Even a recent picture of the princess in one of your ReGen pods. There were a lot more, but I didn't have time to look at all of them."

My blood ran cold. "You broke into one of the master's private suites?"

A strained silence settled over all four of us as we waited for Smith to explain herself.

"No. I did not break in. I was invited."

"What?" I saw red. I knew Master Gee. He was a sadist. He kept slaves and did not treat them well. He was a monster. If he hadn't been one of the original founding members of Trinity, he would have been kicked out years ago.

Decades.

I grabbed Smith's elbow, reaching for the clasp on her cloak. "Did he hurt you? God, did he touch you? Talk to me. Tell me."

She wrenched her arm out of my hold. "What does that matter? I had a job to do and I did it."

"Fuck. You have no idea what kind of danger you were in. He's a monster."

"Oh, I know. I met Morna."

"Morna?" I did not know this name, but I had not been active in the club for some time.

"She belongs to him. I guess. She isn't allowed to leave

the building without him, but when she tried to go inside, she was ordered to sleep somewhere else."

"Where?" I had a feeling I knew, and I didn't like it one bit.

Smith shrugged. "I don't know."

"None of this makes sense. How did you end up inside his suites?" Kayson, apparently, was the only one thinking with his first brain, rather than the one inside his cock. I was having trouble moving past the nightmares in my memories, visions of Master Gee inflicting pain. The subs wanted the pain, at first. But he usually went too far.

If he'd laid a single finger on Smith, I'd— I'd—

Fuck. I wouldn't do a fucking thing. She wasn't mine. She didn't want to be mine. She was a free agent. She was working on this case and then going home, to another planet. When this was over, I'd never see her again.

"Will you please stop panicking. I heard some things in the subs' lounge that made me suspicious. I talked to Morna and asked her to take me somewhere I could freshen up. She took me somewhere, not sure what was in the room because I only pretended to go in. And then I followed her to Master Gee's suites. I heard her asking to be allowed inside. She said she needed to warn him, that someone had been asking her questions about the princess.

"The guy inside basically told her to get lost. Reminded her that her benevolent master had ordered her to sleep somewhere else, somewhere I gathered was not pleasant."

Smith was right. It wasn't.

"Then I told the guard I had wandered too far and become lost. He invited me to wait inside until someone could escort me back downstairs—because poor, little helpless sub that I am, I couldn't possibly find my way back all by my little, *ittle bittle,* self."

Geros tilted his head to the side. "What are these odd words? Why are you speaking so strangely."

She sighed. "Effect totally lost on you? All three of you?"

I had absolutely no idea what an *'ittle bittle'* was, and neither did my NPU, the neural processing unit programmed to instantly translate every known language in the Coalition and deliver the knowledge directly to my mind. If the NPU didn't understand this term, no one would.

"Fine. I pretended to be afraid to walk back alone. He disappeared. Said he needed to find someone to cover the door so he could walk me back himself. He was actually quite kind."

"Kind?" What the hell was this crazy female rambling on about. I knew that guard. He was a stone-cold killer in the war. He was definitely *not* kind.

"Yes. He was kind to me."

"How were you able to see these images?" My patience was wearing thin. I was about to toss her over my knee and spank her for the risks she'd taken. Alone.

"He is a large man. His footsteps are very easy to hear. I realized the suite was quite large and took the opportunity to look inside Master Gee's office. Or maybe his study. I don't know what you all call it on Viken. I poked around, found the tablet. It turned itself on and an image of the queen was right there. I scrolled through a few more, figured I was out of time and went back to where he left me. Sure enough, he came back and escorted me downstairs."

"You broke into his office and went through his belongings?" Kayson asked. He appeared to be unaffected by her story. At least he could form coherent sentences. "Do you know how dangerous that was?"

"I've done much worse. Believe me. The only thing that spooked me was his cat thing."

"Cat thing?" Geros looked as confused as I felt.

"I don't know what you call it. Some kind of pet. It came in while I was looking around and wouldn't leave. I had to lock it inside the room when I left. Which could be bad. If the creature is truly like a cat, they probably won't think a thing of it. Cats get into odd places all the time. But if not? He will know someone was in his office poking around."

"If you'd been discovered, you would have been killed." Kayson was calm. Too calm.

But he hadn't looked into Smith's eyes as she came, as Geros filled her with his cock. As the device I'd placed over her clit had made her eyes glaze with pleasure. He wasn't the one she'd trusted to take care of her tonight.

No, that responsibility was squarely on my shoulders. And it was by pure chance that she was alive. That, in my estimation, was a complete and total failure.

Apparently, talk of death was the one thing to which Smith had no response. She shrugged. "He's the bad guy we are looking for. Do your thing. Figure out how we're going to get our hands on that tablet and take him alive. He will need to be questioned. I'm exhausted and we have to go back tomorrow night."

"Why would you risk yourself again? We have what we need. We know he's involved." Geros sounded about as excited as I felt. The thought of taking her back into that building, of placing her in danger again was like a pit of darkness gnawing away at my insides.

"We don't want him, Geros. We need his boss. He's a minion, not the leader. We need to go in there and take the rest of those images, and his books, and records, and everything else he has in that suite. We need to get our hands on all of it, because something in those rooms will lead us to his boss, to the top echelon of the VSS."

"Just send in the royal guard. Or notify the queen. She'll have the guards here in minutes," Kayson insisted.

Smith shook her head. "Don't forget there is a traitor inside the palace. If we make that call to the queen, if she sends out the guards, Master Gee will know they are coming before they get out the palace gates. That would give him time to destroy the evidence, escape, or both. And then we are right back where we started."

I hated every word out of her mouth. "She's correct. We have to take him by surprise.

"Exactly. We go in quiet. We take him alive. Then we call the queen." Smith turned away from all of us and walked toward her bedroom.

"I'm going to bed. We can argue about this more tomorrow." Her cloak dragged on the floor behind her, her hair was a wild mess around her shoulders. She looked like a queen herself.

And then she was out of reach, behind a door I couldn't break down, locked tight by duty. Circumstance. Royal orders. Maybe even fate.

8

MAL SAT in the far corner of the room, staring at Smith's closed door like he could knock it down with a glare. Geros had excused himself, strangely quiet about the events of the day. He'd showered and gone to bed.

What the fuck had happened today between these three? What had they done to her?

I sat close to Smith's room and listened as the shower unit went on, then off. I listened to the quiet noises she made getting ready to go to bed. I heard the quiet padding of her footsteps as she walked across the room and climbed into bed.

And I heard her tears. She was not sobbing, more like

riding a set of waves that ebbed and flowed. Cry. Sniffle. Silence. Repeat.

I couldn't fucking take it.

I walked over to Mal and sat opposite him so I could whisper. "What the fuck happened today? She's in there crying."

"I know."

That was it? That was the only explanation I was going to get? "Why is she crying, Mal?"

"I don't know."

"That's a lie." Frustration made my knees bounce up and down over feet that were hopping like little engines. "What happened? Did you hurt her? Was she threatened? Why is she so upset?"

"I promise you, Kayson. I do not know. I was very careful with her. Extremely careful not to touch her or cross her personal boundaries. I stuck to the script until she changed things."

"How did she change things, exactly?" I asked.

"She begged Geros to fuck her in the ass. And he did."

I stood, ready to beat both of them until they needed a ReGen pod. "You did not allow that."

"I did. She begged. She enjoyed herself. She had more than one orgasm and she seemed to be completely fine when we were done with the scene. After that, she took off on her own. I don't know what happened to her during that time. The explanation she just gave us is the only explanation that has been offered. You know as much as I do."

Well, fuck. Mal wouldn't lie. If he said she begged, she did. If he said Smith had enjoyed herself and had more than one orgasm, she had. "Then why is she crying?"

Mal looked up at me and I saw a bit of despair in his eyes. Confusion. "I don't know. I wish I did. I do not."

Smith chose that moment to pitter-patter to the bathing room and turn on the water.

She was up. Awake. "I'm going in there."

"Good luck. Viken females are difficult to deal with. From what I have seen, human females even more so."

I ignored him and his doomsday attitude. Females were.... I didn't know, exactly, but I had a mother and three sisters. Between the three of us, I had the best chance of figuring out what had obviously gone wrong today.

Lifting my hand, I rapped gently on the door with two knuckles.

"Yes?"

"It's Kayson. May I enter?"

If I were one to be deterred by a feminine sigh of annoyance, I would have run for the hills. Fortunately, I was not so easily dissuaded.

"Okay. Come in."

I stepped into her private bedroom and closed the door behind me. Once inside I set the room's system to play some calming music. When she gave me a questioning look, I grinned. "So we may speak in private."

She wore a pale pink shirt that looked large enough to fit an Atlan in beast mode. The hem fell to the middle of her thighs. The front had a V-neck opening and the fabric looked extremely soft. But her legs, those soft, supple legs were bare. I could see the tips of her nipples under the material. I wanted to pounce, but she wasn't mine. And from the sounds of it, there had been enough pouncing already today. "Is this typical sleep attire on Earth?"

"Depends, I guess. It's just an oversized T-shirt. Jersey cotton. It's comfy."

"May I approach?" I wanted to walk straight to her and pull her into my arms, demand she tell me exactly what was bothering her. But that would be stupid, and I was not a stupid male.

"I guess. What do you want, Kayson? I'm tired and I want to go to sleep."

I walked to stand directly in front of her. Her back was pressed to the wall that separated the bathing room from her sleeping chamber. "I want to hold you so you'll feel better and stop crying."

She froze is if I'd burned her. Had I made a terrible mistake? Been too direct?

I stared down at her and waited as she lifted one hand to the base of her throat and gently stroked the exposed skin there. "No sex?"

"On my honor. I only wish to hold you tonight."

I was not sure what I said to ignite her tears, but her dark eyes filled with them. I reached up and wiped them from her cheeks with my thumbs.

"Okay."

"I may hold you?"

"Yes."

Thank the gods, I couldn't endure any more of her suffering.

Gently, I tugged on Smith's elbow, pulling her to my chest. Relief flooded me when she acquiesced and settled her cheek over my heart.

"Talk to me. Tell me what's wrong."

"Nothing. I found the evidence we needed. All we have to do is track down Master Gee and let him lead us to the traitor at the palace."

"I'm not talking about the mission, my lady. I'm talking about you."

She pushed against my chest but I wasn't about to let her go, not when she was so brittle the slightest stress would break her. Had Mal pushed her too far at the club? "What happened today? Were you in danger?"

"A little."

"Did Mal...did he..." Fuck, how was I supposed to ask such a delicate question? Did he push you too far? Did he treat you like a true sub when you clearly are not?

"No. He didn't touch me. And what happened with Geros..." She looked up at me and I inclined my head just a bit to acknowledge that I knew what had happened between them. "That was all me. Mal had nothing to do with it."

"Very well." I rubbed her back slowly. She seemed jumpy as a cornered beast. "I will stop asking for explanations. You are female." That, in my opinion, was explanation enough for this display of raw emotion. Tears.

"Give me a break, Kayson. What do you want me to say? I'm fine. I don't even know why I'm crying." She was shaking.

"Shhhh. Rest. There is nothing else we can do tonight. You don't have to do anything but let me hold you."

"You don't have to do that. I'm a big girl. I can take care of myself."

"What if you don't have to?"

"In what universe?"

"This one."

I loosened my hold, my gut clenching at the distant look in her gaze, a mental barrier she put between us. She shuddered, her gaze distant. She was shutting down. Shutting me out. Like she'd done with everyone in her life? I'd listened to her conversation with Mal. She never kept a lover for long. She hasn't said anything about her family. Did she have a family? Was she alone in the universe?

There had been sadness in her statements. Disappointment and hurt buried so deeply I doubted she was aware of how much it consumed her. Anger rolled through me.

She would never feel like this again, if she were mine. Which she was not.

Right now, she needed someone to hold her. She needed to cry. Perhaps she needed to scream and beat my chest until she had no strength left in her arms.

I had no idea what she was thinking or feeling or needing. But I wanted to know. I wanted to know everything about her, inside and out. Her heart. Her dreams. Her past. And I would learn nothing until I broke through the barrier she had around her heart.

I wanted to be her safe place.

I pulled her closer, needing to feel her softness against my hardness. Needing to feel her heart beating against my chest. Needing to know she was safe.

"I won't hurt you," I whispered into her hair. "I swear it."

She shook her head but didn't push me away. I wasn't going anywhere. She wouldn't be alone anymore. At least not when she was with me.

"I won't leave you in pain. A male's place is to protect and provide for his female."

Her voice was shaky. "You're not my male."

I held her tighter and a thought came to me unbidden.

I want to be.

I stumbled over the idea and realized it was true.

I wasn't a twenty-year-old fool any longer. I would be careful with Smith. Find a way to give her what she needed. Seduce her. Convince her to stay. To be with us. Our mate.

She stilled, then settled against my chest, melting against me. Trusting. Allowing me to shelter her. It was a start.

I lifted her in my arms, carried her to bed. I pulled the

blanket up to cover us and folded myself around her like a shield.

She had come to Viken for one reason, to track down and expose the leader of the VSS. When we'd left the palace, that was all that mattered.

That was not all that mattered to me, not anymore.

9

S mith, Club Trinity

I CAN DO THIS. I can.

Go back to that room, Mal's *special* room, where I'd begged Geros to fuck me harder, moaned with pleasure as Mal flogged me, and turned into a wild animal. The pain shot through me like raw energy, an aphrodisiac that made me insatiable. Crazed with need.

That had to be what happened. I'd lost control and lost sight of the mission objective. Not that I would admit that to the two males walking with me today. This time it was Kayson who accompanied us. Geros had insisted, practically jerked the weapons and gear from Kayson's hands.

As if he could not bear to be locked in that room with me again.

Noted. Won't ask. Hurt like hell, but I wasn't about to talk about that, either. Or about the way Kayson had melted my heart into a puddle last night. An oozy, bleeding raw messy puddle. I didn't give my heart away. Not for a long time. I rarely allowed anyone to see any vulnerability, let alone cry and cry and snuggle under the covers for hours with a complete stranger. Sure, he was tall, sexy, had rock hard muscles and a smile to die for. But still.

What. The. Hell. Was. Wrong. With. Me?

So, Geros would be the look-out today. Kayson drew the short straw, apparently. And then there was Mal. He was the only reason we got through the door. He really didn't have a choice in whether or not to be here with me. But he did have full control over whether or not he touched me.

Which he hadn't. Not off script. Not once.

Geros fucked me and loved it. Kayson crawled into bed with me and held me all night. And Mal? He barely spoke to me and acted like I had bubonic plague. Real confidence builder, that one.

Today we were going to do a simple scene—no going off script today—and then sneak off and break into Master Gee's suites, the three of us. Together. I would wind my way back through the hallways and turn on the beacon in the ankle bracelet I wore. The guys would find me. But first we had to play our parts so I could get back into the lounge. No submissive was allowed into the salon until after serving their Dom. Or Domme. Some of the people giving orders around here were women—females, as my guys called us. Not a lot, but a few.

A quick glance at the guarded door showed a pair of male subs entering the lounge. They were laughing and joking and looking very well taken care of. Something inside me softened a bit at the sight. Earth was so damn uptight. It shouldn't matter who you fell in love with. Male. Female. One person...or three.

Shit. Don't even think it, Carmen. Do. Not.

"Mate?" Mal opened the door to the private room the club had prepared for us—again—and waved his hand indicating I should enter first.

My choice. My body.

Pumpkin. Pumpkin. Pumpkin.

God. I stepped inside and the smells assaulted me. I hadn't realized this room had a particular scent, but my pussy knew. The little bitch was wet before Mal closed the door.

My Dom, Mal, led me to the same table he'd tied me to the day before. This time, I faced him and he lifted me so that my bottom was on the very edge. He ran his hands from the outer edges of my hips down to my ankles, the heat of his touch like being dipped in a hot bath.

"I am going to place your feet in these two braces. I am going to tie them in place and spread your legs wide so I can see that glistening pussy."

Oh god. *Yes!*

"After that, I am going to place a plug in your bottom because you like that, don't you, mate? You like having something in your ass, stretching you open."

Why lie? He already knew the truth. This was part of the script I had agreed to. Besides, it sounded better and better every second. "Yes, Sir."

He ran his hands down to the bottoms of my feet and tickled me, just enough to make me jump and squeal in surprise. His smile was surprised and quick to disappear. "Are we ticklish, mate?"

"Yes, Sir."

He glanced over his shoulder to where Kayson stood looking unsure about what the hell was going on. I didn't know either, but this was going to be the last time I was in this position and I decided I didn't want to waste of moment of it. Fuck my guilt and fuck these Viken males. Fuck the people I could feel gathering around the outside of the room to watch Master Mal at work. I was going to feel good, for myself. Because I could. Self-love. My therapist had been preaching self-care at me for the last three years. I never quite got it. Today I finally did.

"Kayson, please place my mate's feet into position and strap down her ankles."

Kayson moved quickly, but silently, as Mal held my gaze. I couldn't look away as the straps tightened just enough to keep me in place. I was at Mal's mercy. Again.

I breathed them in, both of them. Mal. Kayson. I'd spent the night in bed with Kayson and I could still smell him on my skin. Mal watched as I lifted my forearm to my nose and breathed him in. I'd never been this turned on in my life. If either one of them blew a puff of air over my clit, I was going to arch up off this table. One touch. Anything.

Instead, he placed his hand on my sternum, between my breasts, and gave a gentle nudge. "Lay back, mate."

I did. He hadn't removed my lingerie this time. Just the cloak. Probably because he'd stared at the white pantyhose and garters I'd added this time for long minutes after I came out of my bedroom. And my new bra? More like frames for my breasts, open in the front, nipples uncovered. I'd gone full-naughty temptress today. Their S-Gen machine was freaking amazing.

"It's time to put something in that perfect bottom."

Oh god.

"You know what I'm going to do. You know it's going to feel good. I won't hurt you. My mate will enjoy the feeling of being plugged and filled."

Well, I did. He wasn't wrong about that.

He pulled a plug from the nearby shelf and twirled it in front of me. "When I push this in, you will feel the burn, but I will make you forget the pain with this..." He pressed the plug against my clit, rubbed it through the crotch of my panties. "...and Kayson's tongue."

"What?" Kayson was staring at my pussy like a man possessed. Mal had stolen all of my attention, but Kayson seemed hypnotized as Mal rubbed the butt plug up and down the outside of my panties.

And then I remembered he was the one from Sector

Three. Their favorite kink was oral. According to the brief I'd read back on Earth, they would fuck their female with their mouths for hours before filling her with their cocks.

Hours. Jesus fucking Christ.

"Do you like that idea, mate?"

"Yes, Sir." I was panting now. I didn't like it, I needed it.

Mal ripped the seams of the little lace panties I wore and put them in his pocket. "Good. Now I am going to place this plug in your ass and Kayson is going to make you come. You will not come until I give you permission."

Oh, shit. No. I wanted to come now. ASAP. Didn't he get the memo?

"Look at me."

I tore my gaze from Kayson, who still stared at my now exposed pussy. I'd put on the garters and hose hoping Mal would leave them on. Wicked. So bad. But while in Rome...right? This was my chance. No one here knew me. No one would ever see me again. I could give in to the darkest urges I had. The shameful ones. The things I kept buried in dark places. They were rattling the cages in my mind, desperate to get out.

Maybe, after this mission was over, I'd come here again. On my own. Before I left for Earth. I had some vacation time saved. Months of it. I could find one of the Doms in the other room to...

To what? I didn't know. I didn't freaking know.

A smack on my ass brought me back to the moment, the sharp sting going straight to my nipples which were suddenly hard as freaking rocks.

"Smith. Your mind left this room. Look at me. Focus on me."

"Yes, Sir." That was not a difficult ask. Mal was hot, bossy, dominant and freaking gorgeous. I wanted that big plug in my ass. I wanted Kayson's mouth on my clit. I needed more...

"Turn your head and look at Kayson."

I did. He was staring at me. He looked as desperate and on edge as I felt.

"Hold his gaze as I fill your ass. Don't look away. Show him with your eyes everything you feel." Mal moved to stand between my thighs and placed the tip of the plug on my bottom hole. The wet warmth of the lube he had chosen filled me first. Then...he pressed forward.

I moaned. It was a cross between pleasure and pain. He kept pushing until there was a pop as it slid past my inner muscles. Stretching me. Making me burn. The plug was big enough that I knew it was there, but it wasn't Geros filling my ass. It wasn't my man, but for now, it was enough.

Mal spanked my ass again. Once. Twice. He walked up my body and pinched my nipple. It hurt, but he had figured out that I liked a bit of pain. I loved all of it. The burn in my ass, the fact that I couldn't move, was at their mercy. The anticipation of having Kayson's gorgeous, golden-brown head between my thighs. Everything pushed me closer to the edge. I didn't have to think or judge or deny myself anything. Mal was in control now. Mal decided what to do. Not me. The idea was erotic.

Frightening. And a freedom I'd never experienced before meeting him. Before this place.

He pinched my other nipple.

I moaned again. My nipples were hard and achy.

Mal took my hands and raised them up over my head. Once they were well placed, he wrapped something smooth around my wrists, not too tight, but tight enough I wouldn't be able to free my hands. I was completely at their mercy now, tied hands and feet. Unable to move.

Did I want to move?

"Kayson. Feast on her pussy. Don't stop until she comes."

No. I definitely did not.

Kayson moved between my legs. Mal watched, his arms crossed. He was in charge here. My pleasure, and Kayson's mouth, his to command.

Working his mouth up my body, Kayson started with the bottoms of my feet. Ankle. Leg. Inside of my knee. Thighs. I had trouble getting enough air, I was shaking too much.

At last, he licked my clit. I gasped. The gasp became a groan as Kayson lowered his head farther and sucked my sensitive nub into his mouth.

He started with soft strokes, pulling at my clit, making me cry out.

Mal kept his eyes on me as my back arched. Unmoving. Unmoved. So stoic as if none of this mattered. No judgement. Just...command. An order. I was following his orders, and so was Kayson. Doing so allowed me to be honest with my body in a way I'd never known with any other lover.

Kayson swirled the top of his tongue around my clit, teasing the hard nub. My teeth bit into my bottom lip to hold back a scream.

Sensations built inside me as Kayson slowly built my need, his tongue slowly driving me to the edge.

I felt him add fingers to my slit, slowly inserting them deeply into my pussy. I arched my back, moaning loudly. The plug in my ass made me so full, so tight and sensitive, but still I wriggled, trying to take more. My legs were spread, held open. The dark walls were, I knew, transparent. I could feel amber eyes on me, watching with desire. Lust. Envy. The knowledge made me feel powerful, that power like a lightning bolt to my clit. I bucked against Kayson's mouth, hard, the moan that came from my throat not recognizable as human.

"Harder Kayson. Fuck her with your fingers and the plug."

Kayson buried his face between my legs. He was relentless, not stopping his sensual assault. He flicked his tongue over my clit, fluttered it back and forth, and then licked me from my clit to my ass. The plug shifted, and I moaned, still so sensitive from Geros's hard cock. Soon Kayson's mouth again locked onto my clit even as his fingers moved in and out of me in a rough, fast rhythm. He wiggled the plug as well, not taking it out, but reminding me it was there. That I had been stuffed, filled. Claimed. I held onto my sanity by a thread, holding myself back, knowing the release would all the sweeter if I waited for my master's command.

I wanted to please Mal. I wanted him to touch me as well. Fuck me. Fill me up. Why wasn't he touching me?

Why did I care? Shit. I was falling in love with him, wasn't I? Him, and Geros. And Kayson.

I was so screwed.

"Now you may come."

The moment Mal said those words I felt a delicious warmth spread over my entire body. My pussy was the epicenter, a molten volcano waiting to erupt. Kayson opened his mouth and I saw those amber eyes get even darker, if that was possible. His tongue slipped between my swollen lips and lapped up my juices like they were the sweetest honey he'd ever tasted as my inner muscles continued to jump and spasm around his fingers.

When I came back down, Mal was watching me. Waiting. I expected him to tell me to tell Kayson to fuck me now, or maybe move Kayson out of the way and fuck me himself. That's what I wanted him to do. But he stood, walked where my head rested on the bed and kissed the stray tear I hadn't realized was there. He licked the moisture from his lips before speaking to me in the softest tone I had ever heard from him.

"Do you want more, little one?"

"Yes, Sir."

He turned his head to the side and spoke to Kayson, his voice a hard command. "Again."

He turned back to me as he spoke. "Mate, you may

come as many times as you wish. Kayson will not stop until you beg him to do so."

Kayson sucked my clit into his mouth at Mal's words.

I nodded and my eyes closed on their own volition, the pleasure now too much for me to bear. Kayson's tongue was relentless, stroking my clit and then slipping down my entrance to take more. I wanted to know what it would feel like to bury my hands in his hair, pull him tighter to me as he made love to my pussy.

He moved his hands to my ass and squeezed, lifted me and spread me even further. He plunged two fingers into my pussy and slipped the other hand down to the plug, manipulating and tapping it as his tongue circled and flicked, bringing me to the edge of another mind-blowing orgasm.

Again, and again Kayson brought me to the edge and then backed off, the sensations almost too much to bear, the pleasure so intense I was glad I'd recently had an EKG, otherwise I'd be worried about a freaking heart attack.

My pussy throbbed and ached, my clit was engorged and I was sure I was going to die of sexual frustration. My body shook and shuddered, quaking and trembling.

Kayson stopped moving and gently kissed the inside of my thigh. He waited for me to look down at him. Our gazes locked. "Come now, mate. Come all over my tongue."

He leaned forward and pressed his tongue deep

inside my core, his hand moving up and over his head to tease my clit with his fingers.

I screamed as I came. I lost control. Mal was watching. *They* were watching. I was giving Kayson what he loved most, oral sex. A pussy to master and tame. God help me, he was a pussy eating prodigy.

When I was able to think again, Kayson's head was resting on my thigh, Mal's fingers wrapped in the hair at the base of his neck as if Kayson needed physical touch to ground him as much as I did. I was floating. If Mal hadn't tied me to this table, I was sure I'd be on the ceiling by now.

I knew I would be sore, but not in a bad way. I had finally found the passion and heat, the desire and need that had been hidden within me all along. I wanted to give it to them. I wanted to give them everything.

Kayson kissed my thigh before standing but Mal was not done with us. With a controller of some kind that I could not see, Mal lowered the table until my face was even with his hips.

"Kayson, fuck her mouth until your seed rolls down her throat."

So crude. So rude. They were cavemen, both of them. Raw sex with two legs.

God, yes. I wanted that cock. I hadn't been allowed to taste them, not really.

Kayson freed his cock from his pants as Mal freed my legs from the restraints and positioned my body so I was more comfortable. I opened my mouth for Kayson's cock and sucked the head to my lips. I licked a bit of pre-cum from the tip, the hit like nothing I'd felt before.

Seed Power.

Oh, god. It hit my bloodstream like a bolt of lightning. I was going to come again.

The raw scent of his body, the power. He'd been holding back, just as Mal had, but I was going to make him come. I was tied to this table, but I was going to bring Kayson to his knees.

I opened my mouth, sucking the head inside. I hollowed my cheeks and lapped at the slit, drawing another drop of his cum to my tongue.

His cock hardened and his body stiffened. He was about to—

I released him, teased him as he had teased me.

Kayson cursed. Mal chuckled.

With a smile I knew was wicked, I took his cock into my mouth again until the head hit the back of my throat. I wrapped my lips around his cock and suctioned as hard as I could, like I was trying to pull every ounce of cum from his balls. All of him. Like he was mine. His seed. His cock. All of him. Mine. Right now, he was fucking mine and he was going to know it.

"Fuuuuck."

If I hadn't had his cock in my mouth, I would have smiled like the Cheshire Cat.

That was it. He was gone, his body shuddering as I swallowed him down, his seed setting off a blooming heat inside my body that made me come again. I didn't think of my own needs and desires. I had none left but to give him pleasure. I wanted this. I wanted him. I wasn't going to stop until I had conquered him.

Mal watched it all, the dark intensity of his gaze confusing.

When I was done taking the euphoric hit of Kayson's Seed Power, I gave his cock one soft kiss on the tip and pulled my head back to let him go. Kayson tucked himself back into his pants before leaning over and kissing me softly on my temple. He ran his fingers through my long hair as Mal stood like a statue and watched us both come down, our breathing slow. My heart didn't feel like it was about to explode any longer, but I wasn't ready to give up the soft, comforting glide of Kayson's fingers through my hair.

Finally, Mal spoke. "Do you want more, mate?"

Maybe, but I wasn't sure I'd survive it. Physically, mentally or, worst of all, emotionally. Having Geros in my ass yesterday had been hard enough to deal with. But this? With Kayson? After the way he'd held me last night? This felt like a relationship. Emotions getting involved. Things getting messy when I had to go back to Earth and they would all be matched—or at least one of them—to their perfect match. An Interstellar Bride. What would I be then?

Nothing. A distant memory while they all took their perfect woman as a mate.

"No, Sir." I tried to sound strong. Solid. The words were barely a whisper.

Mal nodded and instructed Kayson to take care of me, remove the butt plug and get me cleaned up. He announced that he was going to the master's lounge and Kayson was to drop me off at the subs lounge and meet Mal there once he was finished with me.

Then Mal walked out. Just like that. Gone. He didn't even look over his shoulder.

Don't cry. Don't cry. Don't you fucking cry, Carmen.

Why go to all this trouble and not touch me himself? And why did I care? Why did his rejection hurt this much? I'd known him less than a week. I wasn't his matched mate, his real bride. As an exclamation point on that fact, not one of them had fucked me in my pussy, which, I had to admit, had been one of the parameters I had set for this mission. Never occurred to me Geros would take my ass and Kayson my mouth, instead.

Kayson stepped away and I licked my lips, the smallest bit of his cum making my lips tingle with heat. I felt like a limp noodle on the table. Wasted. I couldn't fight my way out of a paper bag right now, especially with Kayson's Seed Power making me all warm and fuzzy and...horny. If he rolled me over and wanted to fuck me again, I would take him. Both of them. Damn it.

Even if Mal didn't want me, I wanted him.

Which meant it was time to finish this mission and go home before I got my heart broken.

10

MAL AND KAYSON had carefully studied the security system of the club. Mal had drawn maps from memory, based on his years as a member. They had even gone as far as taking pictures of where the guards were stationed on the main floor. But with the Master Gee's suites situated on the third floor of the building, they had to be careful. They were not an innocent new submissive lost in the hallways. There was nothing innocent or submissive about either one of them.

No, if the VSS operative in that suite caught us before we could get the jump on him, Mal, Kayson or I could be killed. Or worse.

There were fates much worse than death.

I was still wearing the white negligee, having just come through the back hallway of the subs' lounge to meet them here. I had no underwear—since Mal had torn the delicate white lace off—and I felt like a first-rate idiot sneaking around the halls with my ass on display. But I guess there were worse things. Not sure what, but if I thought about it long enough, I'd come up with something.

Mal and Kayson caught up to me dully dressed. They even had boots.

Anyone who ever said women weren't tough as nails? Obviously not in this hallway right now. "I'll go first. Once the hall guard sees me, I'll flirt with him. Distract him. Then you two can take him out."

"No."

"No."

Mal and Kayson spoke at the same time, which made me smile. "I do believe your queen told you I was in charge on this mission. This is the easiest way to take out the guard without raising an alarm. He will be pleased to see me. Trust me." This particular guard had been more than impressed with what I might...offer him.

My words caused a rumble from one of the males behind me, but I didn't turn to see which one. I didn't care. I was right. That guard had definitely been inter-ested in what he'd seen in the little red negligee I'd worn last time I was here. This white—no underwear—getup was going to knock him out of his boots.

Just as I'd known they would, the guard called out a

greeting to me as I approached. Too bad he wasn't alone this time. Three guards, one me. This was not part of the plan.

"Back again, little one? Are you lost? What are you doing up here all alone."

"I was looking for you."

He slipped one hand around my waist and the other found its way to caress my ass. His touch was gentle, I had to give him that. But he wasn't mine and I had to force the smile on my lips. Hopefully the goose flesh and shiver that raced over my skin would make him think I *liked* his touch, rather than being repulsed by it.

The two guards had come forward, probably to get a better look at me in the brighter light a couple steps farther down the hallway.

I smiled up at the big guard, batting my eyes and whispering quietly, "I was having some trouble last night. I kept thinking about you and couldn't sleep. I was hoping you could help me, Sir."

"I'd be happy to, little one. But where is your Master?"

"Oh, him?" I pouted as if I were a thirteen-year-old girl who'd just been told she had to give away her pony. "He found someone else. Someone better than me."

The muscled bodyguard wrapped his arms around me and I leaned into him with a long-suffering sigh. He smelled good. And he seemed like a decent enough guy. I could feel him already growing hard against my stomach. But inside, I felt nothing. Absolutely nothing. All I could think about was the fact that two men I *did* care about were right down the hall and, if I didn't get this trained soldier, muscled badass out of their way, someone was going to get hurt.

He looked at the younger male guard. "Cover for me?"

The younger male chuckled. "Have fun."

"Come, little one. I will show you how a true male takes care of his lady." He held out his hand and I took it. It didn't take much to get him to lead me down the hall and around a corner to an elevator. I hadn't noticed on my first trip, but Mal had clearly marked it on the map and assured me that it was our nearest escape hatch if we couldn't go down the stairs.

I walked quietly, even resting my cheek against the big guy's biceps. As I'd hoped, the other guards stayed behind and were now well out of sight.

I glanced to where I knew Mal and Kayson waited in the dark corridor beyond our position. On a silent nod from Mal, I waited patiently as my new friend pushed the down button, his large hand slowly stroking up and down my back in what, in other circumstances, would have been a reassuring gentleness. The elevator door whooshed open. He stepped inside and turned to offer me his hand again. "Come, little one."

I know I looked like a very naughty kitten as I took a step back. "I'm so sorry."

————

KAYSON

.   .   .

THE FLAVOR of her hot pussy lingered on my lips. Smith's taste, her eyes as she'd sucked my seed down her throat like a treat. By the gods, I'd known, last night as I held her in my arms while she slept, that I was going to keep her. Mal? Geros? If they were too stupid to know how perfect Smith was, I would find two other males willing to honor the new kings' tradition of sharing a mate.

I had no idea what either of them thought about the matter. We'd agreed to take the mission, fulfill our duty to the queen and let her go. Return to Earth. Leave us. But now?

I'd seen Mal today, barely able to control himself.

Smith said Mal hadn't touched her, and she'd been correct. But I realized today his restraint was not because he didn't want to touch and explore and conquer. No, I had a feeling it was the direct opposite. Mal wanted her, badly. That much was clear to me now. I knew what lust looked like. Desire. *Need.* Mal needed Smith as much as I did. The trick would be forcing him to admit it.

I watched Smith sashay down the corridor toward not one, but *three* guards. Her round, perfect ass beautifully —and barely—covered by the softest, sheer fabric I'd ever encountered. She looked like a phantom, a goddess come to life to seduce males like me.

And like that fucker drooling all over her.

He put his hand on her ass.

Seeing the male guard put his hands on Smith, treat

her as he might a mate, brought a rage to life within me that I'd never felt before.

My muscles tensed. Mal's hand came down on my shoulder. "Do not. It is the Seed Power affecting your mind."

The Seed Power. Fuck. I knew better. I knew the connection it forged between a male and his mate was rumored to be instant and powerful. I'd never given my Seed Power to any other female. I'd always been careful. I should have been careful today.

Who was I kidding? I wanted my seed in her. I wanted to bind her to me, to make her hunger for me, for my cock, my body. My attention. Above all, I wanted to give her all of them and more. Protection. Care. Love. Children.

God, Geros. He was obsessed with having a family. Children. Finding a mate and binder her to us. He had given his seed to Smith as well.

Perhaps I would only need to replace one hard-headed idiot to create the family Geros and I both wanted. With Smith. I would fight to keep her. Win her heart. Do whatever I had to do to make her happy. If she would stay. She just had to stay on Viken.

I took a deep breath, tore my gaze away from that fucker's fat hand on Smith's perfect ass, and readied himself for the task at hand. My heart pounded in my chest as I moved towards the corner where I knew Smith would be waiting with the large male she had lured away. The male touching her and stroking her like she was his.

Fuck. That.

I agreed with Smith's assessment. Of the three guards currently on duty, he was, by far, the most dangerous. One soldier recognized another easily. I wondered, briefly, where he'd been stationed in the war. Perhaps we had even fought on the same battlefield against the Hive.

But then I heard him call our Smith *little one,* that was the end of that. I didn't care if he'd taken out an entire legion of Hive Soldiers. He had his hands on my mate. Unacceptable.

I knew what I had to do. I steeled himself, took one last deep breath, and then leapt around the corner.

The guard stood dead center in the elevator, his hand extended to Smith.

She took a step back. "I'm sorry."

Sorry? She was apologizing to this asshole?

I fired my ion blaster. Twice. It wouldn't kill him, but he'd wake up later with a massive headache, his body aching all over. He deserved worse for touching my mate. My Smith.

The guard crumpled to the ground. I stepped inside and active a timed delay used for evacuations. No sense sending him to the ground floor where he would be found.

The doors closed on him and I watched him disappear with satisfaction a living, breathing thing heaving in my chest. The feeling nearly exploded out of me when Smith walked to my side and allowed me, *me,* her *mate,* to pull her close and hold her.

"He'll have a headache when he wakes up."

"He wasn't a bad guy."

I growled. "He touched you."

"Kayson. The Seed Power. Get your head on straight." Mal looked us over, his gaze lingering on my hand where it rested on her hip, at her arm where it circled my waist as she held me in turn. His permanent scowl deepened. "Let's go. We have two more guards and Master Gee to deal with."

———

Mal

I raced down the corridor, my adrenaline pumping. I ran faster, dodging ion blasts as I went. I reached the door at the end of the corridor and was met with physical force by one of the two guards. The second had his blaster drawn and pointed down the hall at Kayson who was directly behind me.

Holding onto the guard in front of me, I shoved both of our bodies into the second guard. His blaster fired but the shot hit the ceiling and then...Kayson was on him.

Kayson attacked. The two of them wrestled for control of the blaster, but Kayson eventually gained the upper hand. He managed to disarm the guard and then proceeded to punch him in the face, knocking him out.

Free to focus on my opponent, I yanked him close and slammed my forehead into his face. He crumpled at my feet.

My head hurt, but maybe that would stop the insane thoughts spinning inside my fucking skull. Thoughts about taking Smith, wrapping her in a soft blanket, as I had the first day I saw her, and taking her as far away from this fucking city—and this club—as we could get. Thoughts about keeping her.

Since the moment we'd walked into the club, I'd been pawed over and flirted with every moment I wasn't with Smith. I'd been propositioned. Baited. Seduced. None of them knew me. None of them cared what I did outside of the walls of this club. All they wanted was a Master. They wanted to use me up and take advantage of my innate need to serve them, to give them what they needed— even at my own expense. And I would. I knew I would. I'd accepted the weakness in myself and quit coming to this place, stopped serving these people who took and took until they made me leery. Cautious. Until I held myself back and didn't become involved in other people's lives.

Until Smith. I hadn't touched her. I knew I could. Fuck, she'd invited me to. But I couldn't do it. If I started, I wouldn't want to stop. I wouldn't be able to stop until she gave me everything.

Smith appeared, now that the fight was over. Kayson moved quickly to the woman he was falling in love with, beckoning her to come to him. Which she did. She moved in close, so her shoulder touched his arm. Contact. Comfort.

It fucking pissed me off and I knew it shouldn't. An irrational part of me wanted to pull her away from him, lay her down on the floor right here, right now, and fuck her until she screamed my name. I wanted to claim her. Mark her. Keep her.

Impossible.

"Be careful." Smith whispered the words to me as I used the unconscious guard's hand on the scanner and opened the door.

Kayson picked up the other guard's ion blaster and nodded as he pushed Smith behind him. She made a small noise of protest but didn't fight him. Smart girl. No fucking way she was walking into this room first, queen's orders or not.

I could feel the nervous energy radiating off Smith, yet she put on a brave face and stepped forward with us, staying close.

The door was old, the hand scanner deactivating the lock but not sliding the door open. This one was on hinges like the more primitive parts of Viken. Outside of the few large cities, most people preferred to live a much simpler life.

I swung the door open on silent hinges. A blast of cold air poured out of the dark room before us. I swallowed hard, desire to take a step back and carry Smith away from danger rising in my throat. I glanced at Kayson, trying to gauge how my friend was holding up. Kayson was an experienced fighter. His gaze was alert, his posture loose and ready as he looked into the darkness. Smith stood firm behind him and nodded for me to continue.

Moving silently, I stepped into the hallway, expecting a surprise attack at any moment. I paused, listening for any sound in the darkness. Nothing. My feet moved slowly as I crept further in. Somewhere down the hall, I heard the low hum of a machine of some sort, but nothing else. I expected to hear voices, weapons being drawn, but no one was here. As my eyes adjusted to the darkness, I saw that the hallway split in two directions. I motioned for Kayson to follow and began to move down the left path.

It was too fucking quiet.

A loud crash came from the hallway behind Kayson.

Smith!

The sound of metal clanging against metal echoed off the walls. An icy chill ran down my spine. I rushed back the way I had come, Kayson at my side. Before we took two steps a man emerged from the darkness, a blaster in his hand.

"Where are my guards, Mal?" Master Gee stood with a blaster pointed directly at my head. He wouldn't miss, not like the amateurish guards we'd dispatched at the door.

"Alive." That was all I would give him.

A feminine scream of rage echoed through the room behind him.

How had we lost Smith and not noticed? Fuck. This was my fault. She should have been between us where we could keep an eye on her.

Master Gee moved the blaster, indicated that we should move toward the sounds of a physical altercation.

I tensed to run to Smith, to help her. I saw Kayson make a similar move.

An ion blast hit the floor directly in front of me. The force created a hole nearly the size of my head.

That thing was set to kill. Maximum power.

"Fuck," Kayson mumbled under his breath. He knew what the damage meant just as I did.

"Don't even think about it." Master Gee motioned with the blaster, indicating Mal and I should move farther into the room. Once inside he nodded to a plush sofa. "Sit. Don't fucking move or you die."

"Where is she?" I didn't care if I died. Not if it meant Kayson could get to Smith and get her out of here.

As if on cue, Smith yelled several more times. No words, more sounds of rage. A male voice came through as well, cursing. Loud thuds indicated Smith was putting up a fight.

Our captor chuckled. "Brought me a feisty one as well? This is turning into a very good night."

"If she's hurt, I will rip you apart." I looked at Kayson. We'd been in enough fights together he would know what I was asking with the slight movement of my eyes in Master Gee's direction.

Kayson shook his head. I squeezed down my rage and fought for patience. Smith was alive. We could hear her. Charging this fucker might be our only option, but I would save it for a last resort.

"You are in no position to make threats."

A buff young man with a buzzed head and a tattoo

peeking out of the collar of his shirt stepped over to stand in front of Master Gee. "Can I break her, boss?"

"Amok, really? Took two of you to handle one little girl?"

"Gale has her." The man wiped a smear of blood off his lip. His eye was going to be swollen shut soon, unless they had a ReGen wand handy to heal his wounds. Which they probably did. Still, I was proud of Smith for causing such damage. She was fierce. A fighter. We would get out of this.

"So beautiful you don't want me to get a good look?" The sinister chuckle was back. "No, Amok, I don't think so. This one is mine."

Master Gee yelled, making sure his voice carried out into the hallways. "Gale, bring her to me."

We heard an *oof* of pain from Gale.

"Little bitch!"

Our captor laughed and motioned with his blaster toward the dark hall. "Bring her out, Gale."

Gale appeared from the hallway dragging Smith along by the wrist, a bruise already forming on her cheek. Her eyes were wild but clear. She wasn't panicked, she was thinking. She looked regal, like a queen. Her hair was in disarray, she had blood on her knuckles and her incredibly sexy little gown had ripped, leaving her all but naked. Yet, she stared down our captor like she was the one holding the blaster. She had never looked more perfect.

My stomach knotted. Fuck. I wanted her. I'd tried not

to, but it was too fucking late. I had tried to remain unaffected by her charms. Geros has insisted that Kayson come to the club tonight because he'd known he wouldn't be able to keep his hands off her. Now I understood his struggle. I wanted her. I wanted to taste every inch of her skin and bury my cock in her wet heat.

I wanted to keep her. Just like Geros and Kayson. And like them, I was sure to be disappointed. But first, we had to get out of here alive.

Her gaze moved from Master Gee to Amok, then to Kayson and me. She took a step toward us, only to have Gale wrap his arm around her neck from behind, pulling her back against his chest. Her hands flew to his forearm, clawing at him, trying to breathe.

"She dies, I will take a year to kill you." My tone was cold as ice in winter. Gale smiled at me but didn't loosen his hold.

Smith fought, kicked and threw her body from side to side. Kayson rose to his feet but a blaster shot stuck his thigh and he fell to one knee.

Fuck. Time to rush him and fight our way out of here. Gale and Amok would be easy to take out. The real threat was Master Gee.

I looked from Smith to Master Gee and found his blaster now pointed squarely at Smith. "Move and she dies."

I froze in place, not willing to put her in even more danger. She was still fighting, which meant she was still alive.

And then, her body went limp in Gale's arms. Unsure of what to do, the younger guard loosened his hold and watched her limp body slide to the floor. She didn't move. She didn't breathe. Her face was covered with her hair and not one strand changed position. Her chest did not rise and fall. She was perfectly still. Gone.

Something inside me broke.

Gale moved toward us, stepping over her body like he was leaving behind a piece of trash.

Rage consumed me. "I'm going to strip your skin from your bones and watch you bleed."

Master Gee laughed and shot Kayson in the other leg because he could.

And then he turned to me.

11

THANK GOD. I thought that buffoon was never going to leave. I can only hold my breath for so long, and this idiot had pushed me to my limit.

Still, I didn't move too quickly. I moderated the air coming into my body so no one would notice the slight rise and fall of my chest. Warmth flooded me at the vehemence of Mal's threat.

I'm going to strip your skin from your bones and watch you bleed.

Not exactly poetry, but I'd take it. Maybe Mal wasn't as indifferent as he'd seemed.

I'd never had a man be so protective, so concerned about me. Sure, I'd worked with partners before, but I'd not made the mistake of sleeping with any of them. I'd had Colleagues. Acquaintances. Casual friends.

I kept my work out of the bedroom.

Mal sounded like his heart was literally being ripped from his chest. Like he cared about me. Maybe far more than I had realized or hoped. Hope was generally in short supply in my system. I didn't like to waste it on dreams I knew would never come true—such as being loved and adored by three gorgeous aliens who were absolute animals in the bedroom.

Well, at least two of them were. Maybe if I had enough time, I could break down Mal's resistance and he'd fuck me, too. Or maybe not. Maybe I'd stick to my vacation plan, spend some time here and find a nice Dom downstairs that wasn't a psychotic asshole like Master Gee.

Whole lotta maybes rolling through my mind for a girl who's supposed to be dead.

Damn Mal and his anguish, because that little bitch, hope, stirred to life inside me. As hard as I tried to talk her out of making an appearance, she refused to die quietly.

Was I falling in love? With all three of them? Was that even possible? Perhaps. A mother could love three children. A man could love three siblings. Three pets. Three friends. Why not three men? Males. Aliens.

Jeez, just shut the hell up and get up off the floor.

Once I had enough oxygen in my system, I opened my eyes and assessed the situation. I'd purposely made sure to fall with my hair covering my face like a sheepdog's would. Now I looked out through the strands to find Mal and Kayson held at the point of a blaster with two other jerks blocking them from moving to either side.

Kayson was curled in on himself, clearly in pain. I'd heard the blaster go off twice. Had Gee shot Kayson? Shit. And now he stood over Mal, a blaster aimed at Mal's head.

"Why did you break in here?"

"Seemed like a nice place."

"Hit him." Master Gee gave the order but it was Amok who wielded the whip. The sharp snap nearly broke my self-control. Mal's groan of pain made me force back tears. Everything was going wrong.

We were supposed to be doing the questioning here. Guess Master Gee hadn't read the memo.

I glanced at Mal. He was looking at me. Really looking.

"That's right. That dead female means nothing. I'll go downstairs and bring up three more submissives if that's what it takes to get you to talk. I'll have Gale choke them to death while Amok whips you. Doesn't that sound like fun?"

"To a psychopath."

"Or a sadist. After all these years together, Master Mal? You know I'm both." Master Gee laughed as Amok brought the whip down on Kayson this time. Kayson barely jerked in response. The pain of his injuries had to be extreme for him to barely react.

Mal held my gaze for one more second, then looked away. He knew. He was the only one in this room who was paying attention.

Of course he was. The mind reader. The man who seemed to know me better than I knew myself. The one who refused to touch me.

Damn it. The little flame of hope flickered but didn't go out.

Guess I'd better survive this disaster and work on my Seducing Mal plan of attack. I was not leaving this planet without having him at least once. Now that I'd let out my inner horny bitch, she was greedy, too. And I was okay with that. More than okay. I was tired of apologizing for what I wanted or needed out of life. D.O.N.E. Assuming we survived this fiasco.

Master Gee and his goons were idiots, regardless. No one had checked my pulse. They were ignoring me like I was a sack of potatoes.

Never leave an enemy at your back, gentlemen. Never.

But I was just a helpless little submissive. No reason to pay attention to me.

Mal and Kayson were both alive. I intended to keep it that way.

I took an incredibly slow, deep breath and prepared for the fight of my life. Three of them, and only one of me. Master Gee, Amok and Gale. Add in a whip and a blaster. And all three experienced fighters. I was quite sure they shared one goal as well—make sure , none of us left the room alive.

The smell of burned flesh and fresh blood filled my lungs. Mal's blood. Kayson's burned flesh.

No. Not okay.

Moving silently, I got to my feet and charged forward. I jumped Master Gee from behind and grabbed his blaster gun. Feeling the cold metal in my hands, I twisted it out of his hands and hoped it landed in Mal and Kayson's general direction. I jumped off Gee's back and threw a hard right jab into Amok's face before he could get his whip arm back to strike. The impact of my fist against his jaw hurt like hell but heard the crack of his teeth. I spun around and kicked Gale in the stomach, knocking him back before he could grab me from behind. Not again, asshole.

I heard the air rush out of his lungs as he fell to the ground.

Mal and Master Gee were rolling on the floor, trying to kill one another. I moved quickly, dodging Amok's and Gale's punches and kicks while waiting for the right moment to strike.

Amok backed off and I took the opportunity to go for Gale's throat. Direct hit, dead center in the windpipe. He doubled over and dropped onto his ass, hands reaching for his throat as if he could somehow un-collapse the broken shit in there.

He'd tried to kill me first. I felt badly, but then I remembered their fancy ReGen pods.

He would live. Unfortunately.

Kayson called out a warning. I heard the snap of the

whip before I felt it, the sharp sting, a slice of pure fire across my back. The pain was excruciating. Should have been debilitating.

My entire body flooded with rage. Raw, animalistic rage. I turned on Amok, ignored Kayson pulling himself on his elbows toward the discarded blaster. Amok was pulling his arm back to strike me with his whip a second time.

No you fucking don't.

"You're going to die for that."

It was too easy. Or maybe I was just moving in a different time and space dimension for a few seconds. Somehow, the world went into slow motion. I saw the whip arc toward me. I stepped in front of it, the loud crack sounding on the floor where I'd been standing less than a second before. I ran toward Amok. Jumped in the air to land a sidekick but a flash of light made me pull back as Amok's body flew backward.

Just as quickly as things changed, time was normal again. I turned to see Kayson holding the blaster that had ended Amok. He turned slowly, took aim and fired.

"No!" Master Gee's denial rang through the room like he was a child who'd just has his favorite toy taken away.

But instead of a toy, it was Mal he'd lost control over. Mal stood over him looking at the rather large, burned section of Master Gee's face and neck. He turned to Kayson.

"Thanks."

Adrenaline coursed through my veins and I knew my

entire body was trembling with aftershock. The lash on my back was on fire, but Kayson had turned shockingly pale. The wounds on his legs were horrific, burned to the bone on both thighs. But at least they weren't bleeding. If they hadn't instantly sealed, he would be dead already.

I leaned down and put my hand on his cheek. He looked at me but there wasn't much more than the glaze of agony in his eyes. "Safe?"

"Yes. I'm safe. Thank you. You saved me."

He seemed to fade a little after he processed my words.

"Stay with me, Kayson. We need to get you into a ReGen pod. Okay. Just stay with me."

He closed his eyes but when I place my hand in his and squeezed, he held on.

I looked up at Mal. "Are you alright?"

He had his boot heel on Master Gee's throat, just in case the asshole decided not to stay down. "Are you?"

I nodded. "A bit of a headache from master-squeeze over there—" I indicated Gale's now dead body. "But I'll live. I've had worse."

"Not again."

I wasn't sure exactly what he was referring to—there were a lot of options here—so I let it go. We had bigger problems. "Kayson is hurt really bad."

I looked at the bastard who had shot Kayson, conspired to kill a four-year-old and tried to kill Mal.

"The mark on your back. I failed to protect you. I am sorry."

"It's fine."

"You are in pain. You were nearly killed."

What's a girl to do when the man you think you might be in love with looks at you with eyes that sad? That full of self-loathing and shame for something that was not his fault?

I lied. Which I hated, but I wasn't going to break down, cry my eyes out and sob like a baby because one of these assholes tried to kill me. Wasn't the first time. So why was it so much harder to deal with here? With them?

That hope bullshit. That's why.

"I am not in pain. The sting has faded. We won today, we took him alive. That was the goal, our mission, and we did it."

Count on them? Rely on them? Love them? No. Doing that and then going home would hurt worse than dying. At least with dying, I'd be dead. At least, I thought it would. And if I weren't, if some version of heaven or hell did exist, it's not like I'd come back and tell anyone.

Mal slipped his communicator from his pocket so he could contact Geros. All according to plan.

The pressure on my hand released. Kayson was unconscious.

Shit. Not entirely according to plan.

Mal closed the comm, blinked slowly and took a step toward me. I was up and checking on Gale and Amok. Didn't want any fake dead guys springing up to attack me. Never turn your back on an enemy, remember?

I took a step back, keeping my distance. If he touched me right now, I'd crumble like a dry cookie.

His words were like a punch in my gut—or a knife in my heart. "You are, indeed, the highest quality of female I have ever encountered. You saved us today."

"No. This was a team effort."

"You are hurt."

"I'm not."

"The blood on your lip and cheek would suggest otherwise." His tone dropped deeper as if the small amount of blood dribbling into my mouth was of great concern. I'd been hurt worse on the elementary school playground.

I wiped the blood away and shrugged. "Seriously. It's no big deal."

"Mal?" Geros's voice came through the comm unit, saving me a longer, more painfully awkward conversation.

"Here."

Geros's reply was short and to the point. "Four minutes until the swarm of guards arrive. The royal family has been notified as well. We are expected back at the palace immediately."

"Kayson requires a ReGen pod," Mal insisted.

"I told the queen. They are sending a medical transfer unit to pick him up. Best pods on the planet are in the palace."

The comm went dead. I walked to the cabinet where I'd found the tablet containing the digital images of the queen and princess and lifted the damning device from its resting place in its box. Once again, the movement activated the screen, an image of Princess Allayna in her ReGen pod prominently displayed. I held it up so Mal could see it.

"Here is the evidence of Master Gee's involvement in the attempt on the princess's life."

Mal was watching me. I ignored him, walking toward Master Gee, who had recovered enough to lift his head. He had watched me as I removed the device from its hiding place.

I stood over him. I wanted to crush his balls under my boot, but my feet were bare and I didn't want to feel the squishy little fuckers with *any* part of my body. "We know there is a traitor in the palace. If you tell us who it is, the kings might spare your life."

He spit a mouthful of blood on the floor and stared at me. No luck. "I'm a dead man already. You won't get anything out of me."

12

S *mith, Viken United, Four Days Later*

WE'D BEEN BACK on Viken United for four days. The royal guards had stormed the room, taken our prisoner and removed the corpses of Gale and Amok. Once that was done, we ransacked the place. Everything Master Gee had in those rooms—except the tablet, which I had handed to Queen Leah myself—were now in boxes that had been taken somewhere to be combed through and inspected. Turned out Gee had another property outside of the city. They'd torn that one apart as well.

So far, Master Gee had not given them any information.

Which should have frustrated me, but hope was ruining everything. The queen didn't want me to leave until the insider at the palace had been caught. Which was fine with me. I didn't want to leave. I wanted to stay. I wanted Geros and Kayson and Mal to be mine for real. Not just this painful charade we were putting on for everyone in the palace.

I'd been so sure I'd be able to play this part without falling in love with them. I'd been so wrong. I wanted to stay with them for the rest of my life.

I should have known better. I had karma to keep me on my toes. It was all I could do to keep myself from crying, because I didn't want to leave, and I didn't want anyone to know how much I was hurting. I couldn't bear the thought of any of them looking at me like I was weak. Or asking me to stay out of pity.

Kayson had healed in three days and we'd all celebrated together with a feast and wine and the little princesses dancing around the room in fancy gowns. Allayna was healed and had no memory of what had happened to her. She was a happy, rambunctious four-year-old with three big daddies that spoiled her rotten.

But it was the little one that had truly stolen my heart. She was quiet but cuddly. She went from one daddy to the next and snuggled into their arms like it was the best place in the world to be.

I'd sipped wine and watched the royal family smile and touch and love one another.

And my heart had nearly shattered into a thousand pieces of want and a thousand pieces of despair. I went to bed alone. Every night. Four nights I could have been with my mates, if they were mine.

Which they weren't.

Apparently, my boss had already contacted Queen Leah and asked when she was going to send me home. He had work for me to do. Which was depressing to even think about.

I wanted to scream and curse, I wanted to beat the walls with my fists and pull my hair out. I wanted to rip out the hope, rip out my feelings and transport home without every cell in my body yearning for what I couldn't have.

The wistfulness I'd been feeling for the last two days had turned into a despondency so gut wrenching I couldn't bear to look at them. Every time I closed my eyes, I'd see all three of them, remember how Kayson and Geros touched me. Filled me. Fucked me. The way Kayson's tongue had worked my body until I was an exhausted mess. The way he'd tasted on my tongue. The way Mal knew to do things to me that I never would have known to ask for. The intensity in his gaze as I'd looked into his eyes, an orgasm riding me. I ached for all three of them. I didn't know if was from their magical Seed Power or because I had real feelings for them. Did it matter?

Everything was a damn mess and the fact that we were sleeping in the same apartment, just a few steps away from one another did not help. Not one bit.

Every time I heard their breathing in the darkness, I'd wanted to be in their arms. But I couldn't approach them.

Not when Mal appeared to be actively avoiding me like a was a disease he might catch.

Tonight, I was going to tell them how I felt. I had it all planned out. I would state my desires plainly. I would not cry. I would simply explain that I had developed feelings for them, and I would like to have extra time to explore those feelings. Kayson and Geros, I hoped, would agree to give us a chance. Mal I was not sure about. He confused me. I could not figure out what he wanted from me. One moment his gaze made my body feel like he'd set me on fire, the next his gaze was so cold it was like he'd tossed a bucket of ice water over my head.

I needed to talk to him first. If he wasn't interested, I didn't want to embarrass myself in front of the other two by making an ass of myself in front of him. Rejection was hard enough. Rejection with an audience would break my heart. Because I did want him. His intensity. His dominance. The way he bossed me and made me call him, Sir. Everything he did woke a part of me I'd been ignoring for years. I needed him. Too much.

If Geros and Kayson would agree, I had decided to find another dominant male, maybe from Sector Two--like Mal--to join us.

My boss back home didn't know how long this assignment was going to take. He knew I was helping the queen. That I would be gone as long as I was needed here, be that a week or a year.

But he did expect me to come back. He was even checking my mail and watering my plants. Make that plant, singular. I was not very good at keeping things alive.

Frustration made me bold. I had no idea what the queen was planning, but I knew that I had to do something. I had to make sure that none of them got hurt. I had to make sure that the VSS plan was stopped, and that the princesses were safe.

So I did the only thing I could think of. I walked to the throne room and requested an audience with the queen. I didn't know what I was going to say, but I couldn't spend another day wandering around, aching for alien males I could not have. All three of them had resumed their guard duties and worked strange hours. Which left me a lot of time to think. Too much time.

To my surprise, the guard returned quickly and led me inside with a kind smile.

I stepped into the opulent throne room for the first time, my eyes widening in awe. The high vaulted ceiling, the intricate tapestries, the gold and silver accents - it was like stepping into a fantasy world. The floor was a glossy marble, reflecting the light from the many candles and chandeliers that hung from the ceiling. At the far end of the room, four ornate thrones perched atop a dais. The first throne, the largest and most elaborate, was for the queen. I could only imagine her regal splendor as she sat upon it. The three other thrones, smaller but still quite luxurious, were for the three kings. Each throne was made of gold and encrusted with precious gems, the backs of the thrones decorated with intricate carvings of the royal crest.

The thrones were intimidating. Massive. And empty.

The guard turned on his heel and left me standing alone in the cavernous space. I turned in a complete circle, wondering what the heck I was supposed to do now.

"Smith! Over here." Queen Leah's voice echoed. I had to work to locate the source. I passed through an archway nearly as tall as the two-story home I'd grown up in and walked out into a courtyard.

I stepped into the garden and the beauty of the flowers and plants took my breath away. The vibrant colors danced around me, and the sweet scent of the blooms filled the air. Everywhere I looked, there were exotic plants I'd never seen before.

In the center of the garden, a lovely woman with red hair stood with a small blonde girl, about two years old. She was pointing to the different plants and flowers, telling the little girl their names. I couldn't help but smile, watching them together. The woman's face was full of joy, and the little girl's eyes were wide with wonder.

The two of them were so peaceful in the midst of the colorful blooms. I stood there for a few moments, taking it all in. It was easy to forget that the queen's other daughter had recently healed. Or that the queen herself had been threatened and targeted by assassins multiple times. She was the glue that held the royal family together. Without her, or her daughters, the three kings might not stand so solidly together.

I had learned more of their history the past days. The three kings were identical triplets, separated at birth and sent to the three warring sectors of Viken to learn and grow. The idea was to unite them when they were grown, each familiar and loved by the sector where they had grown up. The one hang-up had been finding an heir all three sectors would accept after their deaths.

And so, the story goes, the three kings were matched to Leah, the gorgeous human woman sitting in this garden with me, and all three had filled her with their seed within an hour of their meeting. That way, no one would ever be able to argue who her true father was, or which sector the princess belonged to. Princess Allayna was truly a child of all three of them. And now, so was Lilliana. As the kings were identical triplets, even genetic testing would not yield results.

The Viken Sector Separatists profited greatly from the ongoing Viken wars. They had spent the last four years trying to disrupt the fragile new peace, kill the queen before she could produce an heir. And now, they were targeting the little princesses as well.

Master Gee was one of them. But he wasn't the top of the chain. I'd been waiting to find out if the interrogations would yield any new information, but there had been nothing so far.

"Don't be a stranger. Come in. Come in." The queen motioned me forward.

"This courtyard is beautiful." And it was. I could understand why the queen spent time here.

Leah smiled at little Lilliana, taking a flower from the little girl's hand. "Thank you, lovebug. This is perfect. It's very yellow. Can you find a red one?"

The little girl clapped excitedly and toddled off on unsteady feet to find her mother a red flower.

"She already knows her colors?" I didn't know much about children, but I was impressed.

"Oh, yes. She's every bit as smart as her big sister." The queen watched her daughter struggle to pull a red bloom from a plant for a moment before turning to me. "They are both going to give their fathers hell when the time comes. But I'm not going to warn my mates yet." Her laughter was mischievous and carefree, the sound of a woman comfortable in her life, who knew exactly where she belonged, and with who.

"How is Princess Allayna doing?"

Leah's face was softer than I'd last seen it. The lines around her eyes far less pronounced. She looked like she had finally had some sleep.

"She is doing well. The doctor is keeping her under close watch. He wants to check on her a couple times a day to make sure she doesn't suffer any lingering effects, but her injuries have healed."

"That's wonderful news."

"Yes." The queen wiped a tear from her cheek as Lilliana brought her a bright red bloom. "Thank you love. Can you find mommy one that is blue?"

With a joyful laugh only a child can have, the little girl took off again, running this time.

Once Lilliana was far enough away that she could not hear us, the queen turned to me. "The prisoner has not cooperated. We have learned nothing new. I don't know what to do now. We are tracking all their known associates, of course, but everything is a dead end."

"Smart criminals."

"The worst kind."

Indeed. She was correct. Stupid got caught. Smart, patient bad guys were dangerous with a capital D. "Let me help. Please. I can go through the evidence, look for things your team might have missed. I can interrogate the prisoners as well. Sometimes they'll talk to a woman, admit things they would never admit to a man."

"Oh, no. I could never ask you to do that."

What? "Why not? That's why I'm here. I want to help."

"But Mal said—" Queen Leah stopped midsentence.

"Mal said what? Exactly?" Something ugly bubbled in my blood. I had a feeling I knew where this was going.

The queen turned and took my hand in hers to comfort me.

I was going to kill him.

"I know you don't want anyone to know how hard this has been for you. He didn't tell anyone else. Just me."

"Didn't tell anyone else what?"

"You know, your nightmares. How much you've been

struggling since your close call. I've never been choked out before, but I can't imagine what that must be like."

"Thank you, I appreciate your concern. But I'm okay. I'll feel better if I have something to do to keep myself busy."

She nodded. "I understand. Mal told me you would say that. He's very worried about you." She took a luminescent blue flower from her daughter's small hand and sent her off to find orange.

"He said that? He actually said he was worried about me?" Liar. He wouldn't speak to me. Wouldn't touch me.

Nausea twisted my stomach and I had to take a deep breath in through my nose to keep its contents down. Mal had betrayed me. How the hell did he know about my nightmares? I never spoke of them. Never. I'd learned a long time ago to keep quiet when I slept, nightmares or not. How dare he tell the queen I wasn't fit to continue the mission?

How *dare* he?

"Yes." She nudged me with her shoulder as if we were best friends sharing a secret. "I think he's in love with you."

"Oh, no. He's not. Trust me."

"I know these guys. I've spent years watching them, listening to them. He's in love with you."

No. But there was no sense arguing with the queen of an entire planet, even if she was human, and a woman acting like we were besties. She was still a queen, and I was...what? A poor little girl too traumatized to do the one job she'd been sent to this planet to do?

I was going to kill him with my bare hands.

"Am I allowed to look over the evidence collected from Master Gee's homes?"

"Of course. I was just looking out for you. You've done amazing things so far. This is the closest we've been to finding the leaders of the VSS in years. And I owe that to you."

"Just doing my job."

She told me where they were keeping the evidence. I thanked her and stood. I couldn't sit here with rage roiling in my gut like a stormy sea. It was time to find Mal and show him exactly how a fragile, brittle, little, broken girl could kick his arrogant, bossy, meddling ass.

13

I FOUND him in the training room working with some of the younger guards. The moves he demonstrated reminded me of karate, but with a lot more grappling and wrestling. I watched for about a minute, my rage building equally with my desire.

Why did he have to have his shirt off? Why did his body have to be so god damn perfect? And why was watching him kick these guys' asses making my pussy ache with dozens of very wicked images scrolling through my head like a never-ending porn movie?

Damn him.

I couldn't fuck him, so I focused on the rage.

"Get out!" I walked up onto the training mat and

started taking off my shoes and socks. I glared at Mal as I bared one foot, then the other.

When the Viken fighters he was training looked up at him confused, I repeated the order. "Get out. All of you."

Mal turned to me slowly, the guards watching us closely, his voice irritatingly calm. "What are you doing?"

"I'm kicking your ass." I stuffed my socks inside my shoes and threw them off the side of the mat. In case he didn't think I was serious, I reached for the hem of my shirt.

"You heard her. Training's over."

Damn right it was. I pulled the shirt off over my head and threw it in the direction of my shoes. I had the S-Gen's version of a sport's bra on underneath, bright red, because I freaking liked red, and a pair of stretchy brown pants that wouldn't impeded my movement.

I'd never admit that I wore brown for Mal, for his sector. The color matched his pants exactly. The big jerk. I could not believe I had been mooning over him last night while I was trying to go to sleep. Imagining all the ways I wanted him to—

No. He could take his muscled chest and six-pack abs and shove them—somewhere.

"This isn't necessary. I don't want to hurt you."

"It's very necessary." I danced away from his attempts to grab me and gritted my teeth. "It's been necessary since I stepped foot on this dumb planet. And you already did." I tried a quick jab, just to test his reflexes. And damn, but he was big. And fast. My fist wasn't even close to making contact.

Mal glared down at me. "Are we going to do this now?"

"Yeah." I smiled. "We are." It was all I could do not to lose my shit.

He looked me up and down with a gaze that told me he was just as frustrated and angry as I was. "I thought you were smarter than this."

It was just like him to throw insults around.

I was done with his bullshit. I leaped at him, swinging my fist at his jaw. I was close enough to see the shock on his face as my knuckles grazed his cheek. I tried to swing again, but he blocked my strike and took a step back.

"Smith, you don't want to do this."

"Oh, but I really, really do." I had years of martial arts training, black belts in more than one discipline. I was fit and I was fast. And I couldn't land a single freaking blow.

I tried roundhouse kicks, front kicks. sidekicks. All blocked. I went for his eyes, his throat, his groin. Blocked. He was toying with me. Unless I really wanted to hurt him, which I realized I just couldn't bring myself to do, all I as doing now was using him as a practice dummy. A tall, strong, sexy idiot with no brain cells, practice dummy.

It was a mistake, I knew it before I did it, but I had to get my hands on him, on his skin. I needed to hurt him, just a little, because he'd hurt me. A lot.

I went for a takedown.

He let me. We went down together, me on top of him,

but then he rolled me. As I had expected, he was strong, a lot stronger than I, and we both knew it. He held me down, my chest to the mat. I turned my head so my cheek lay flat and cursed him over my shoulder. "How dare you interfere in my investigation?"

"What are you talking about?" He had me pinned, his torso long enough that I couldn't even move my legs beneath him. I could try to kick him with my legs, from the knee down, but that would just be ridiculous.

And I didn't want to move.

"I talked to the queen."

"Fuck." He loosened his hold on my wrists where they were splayed out above my head in a vee shape. Bad decision. I twisted them, hard, broke free and used my arms to push up and roll onto my side.

He used my momentum against me and rolled me onto my back. He promptly grabbed my wrists again and held them over my head. Just like that he had me pinned again. But this time, his face was inches from mine. Our gazes locked. His cock hardened against my thighs.

Way to add insult to injury. *Now* he wanted me?

"Get off."

"I'm not playing with you anymore," he said. "You needed rest. I told the queen the truth."

"That isn't your decision. It's not your job to take care of me. I don't need a babysitter."

"You don't take care of yourself."

"I do my job."

"You need more than that. What about rest. And fun? And play?"

What about love? Why didn't he ask me about that one?

Because he's not falling for you the way you're falling for him. Duh.

That little voice in my head hurt. Badly. Why didn't he want me? Why? What was wrong with me this time? Maybe I shouldn't have let him flog me. Or let Geros fuck me. Or Kayson and his magical mouth work my pussy until I was begging for release.

Maybe I should have hidden everything inside me the way I always did. But it was too late now. I'd finally shown someone the real me, the kinky, naughty me who needed a bit of pain, who loved sex—all kinds of sex. And what had happened?

The usual. I had to get off this fucking planet.

I slit hope's throat in my mind and went for Mal's jugular.

"You only want to play in the club? Is that it? Watch me fuck everyone but you?"

"Tell me about the nightmares."

Shit. Talk about going for the jugular. "I don't talk about them. They're not real. Tell me why you are so afraid to touch me."

"I am not afraid. That is the role you chose to play."

"I chose it? Lie to yourself all you want to. Coward. You're so full of shit." I glared at him because it was either that or close my eyes, and every time I closed my eyes the weight of him, the press of his cock on my thigh, made me lose my train of thought. "You want to be in charge? You want to take care of me? You're a liar."

"I'm not," he said. He was sweating now, his hands flexing and releasing my wrists.

"You want to go back to the club again? Order some stranger to fuck me this time? Is that what gets you off?"

"No." He was crushing me beneath him. I would cry if he moved. I needed him here. Holding me down. Making me challenge him. Otherwise, I'd run and run and keep running. Alone. Always alone.

"No? What do I need, then? Huh? Tell me, big smart Dom."

"A spanking for running your mouth."

"Oh, no. I'm scared. What else?"

"You need me to rip a hole in your pants and fuck you so hard it hurts."

"Do I? Is that what you think I need?" God yes, I did. So bad. Everything he just said made my pussy hot and wet. My core throbbed in anticipation. My skin was too sensitive, too tight. My heart beat so hard and fast I felt like the poor thing was going to implode.

"Yes." His gaze was locked on mine. Neither of us blinked or moved for one second. Two. Three. Words tumbled around in my brain but I settled on the ones I really wanted to say.

"Do it then. Fucking coward."

The change came over him like he'd flipped a switch. Gone was the gentleman trying not to hurt me as I took wild swings at him. In his place was a very angry male who I'd pushed, *maybe*, just a bit too far.

One moment he was on top of me, our lips so close I could practically taste him—god I wanted to taste him. The next I was on my elbows on the mat, my hips on his lap, ass in the air. He held me down with one arm across the small of my back.

I could have fought my way out of his hold. There were a dozen different moves I could use to escape this, but I didn't want to.

The first swat on my bottom stung, but it wasn't enough. I needed more and he was holding back. Still holding back. I could feel the tension in him boiling up like a pressure cooker with too much steam.

"That all you got? I thought you said you were going to spank me."

He yanked my brown pants down over my bottom and thighs, stopping at my knees. Then he groaned, a finger sliding beneath the tiny slip of thong underwear I'd—maybe accidentally, maybe not—worn just in case. Just. In. Case.

"What are these garments you wear? To torment me?" He slipped one finger beneath the fabric at the top of my bottom and traced the thong's path to my pussy.

"You don't even want to touch me. What makes you think I wore these for you?" Oh, but I had. One hundred and ten percent. I'd known I was coming down here and we were either going to fuck or we were going to fight, I was going to be hurt, and then I was going to beg the queen to send me home early. Now. Like today.

His hand landed on my bare bottom, the sting a delicious fire that spread to my clit. My pussy became wet and achy.

He kept going until I couldn't keep myself under control for another minute. My body was burning up, my orgasm so close. So close. His bare skin on my ass. The quick slap, the lingering heat.

I jerked when his finger trailed over my pussy. "So hot. So wet. I think you like your punishment too much."

I didn't want to lie to him, not ever again. The first one still tasted like acid on my tongue. So I remained silent, until he slipped a finger inside. I moaned. Just a little. Tiny, really. Barely noticeable.

"You like that?" He pushed two fingers deep.

I refused to answer, bit my lip to stop myself from giving in too quickly.

Still filling my pussy with his fingers, his free hand came down on my bare thigh, the sting back again. New. Sharper. Fresh. My pussy had a mind of her own and clenched around his fingers. I would have stopped her if I could have, but she had no fear, no reservations. She wanted more and she wasn't interested in keeping my secrets.

Traitor.

His hand landed on my thigh again, but this time he spoke. "How dare you scare me like that?" *Spank.* "How dare you risk your life?" *Spank!*

Oof. That one was harder.

"How dare you almost die and fucking leave me?"

What?

"Mal, I—"

He lifted me off his lap, turned me settled me on my stomach. In one smooth move he took my pants the rest of the way off. I could just see him over my shoulder, reaching for his cock. "What do you call me?"

That tone in his voice. I knew. I knew instantly. "Sir. I call you Sir."

"Spread your legs. Make room for me to fuck you."

Now? Was this really happ—"

His huge cock pushed into me. Deep. Hard. His hands came down on either side of my head and he leaned over me to whisper in my ear. "Wider."

I did as he asked and he slipped in farther, bottoming out inside me with a bite of pain that made me gasp. His hips settled on my ass, his body a blanket of heat on my stinging bottom and cold back. He covered me and I melted. So good. So hot and sexy and safe.

"Do you like that?"

He was asking me. He always asked me. I realized that now. Mal was taking care of me even as his own frustration and anger had to be boiling inside him.

That fast my rage died, extinguished completely, like a candle dipped in water. Gone.

He was inside me, over me. He was finally talking to me, touching me, showing me what he wanted. What he needed.

"Yes, Sir. It's so good. I need you. I need you inside me." My voice was softer than I'd ever used with him. With any lover. "Please, Sir. Fuck me. Use me."

His entire body shuddered. He settled himself on top of me, holding just enough weight on his elbows so I could breathe. And he fucked me. Hard. Deep. Fast. He was over me and inside me, his arms around me. He was everywhere.

I closed my eyes and became nothing but sensation as his cock moved in and out of my body like a piston. Pleasure built. Fire. I waited for him to tell me to come, for the order that would set me free.

His body tensed. His cock jerked and filled me with cum. His Seed Power. The only one of the three I'd never tasted.

It rushed through me like a flash flood. Unexpected. Fast. Dangerous. If taking drugs felt like this, I knew why it was so hard to kick. This was...bliss.

He rolled off me and turned me on my side to face him. "You did not come."

"No, Sir." I rolled me head on the mat, high on him, and the spanking, and Seed Power.

"Tell me what you need. Why did you not orgasm?"

I smiled. He was so cute. Adorable really. All big and mean and gruff. Mr. Don't Mess With Me. And all along he was a great big softie. The softest softie. Hurt so easily. I would need to be careful with his heart. Very careful.

I reached up and ran my finger over his bottom lip.

He hadn't kissed me yet. Not on his own. Not outside of a scene at the club. I wanted to kiss him. A lot.

"Answer me."

Wait. What was he asking? Right. An orgasm. "You didn't tell me to, Sir."

He groaned and buried his face in my neck. "What am I going to do with you?"

Before I could come up with a smart ass reply his fingers closed over my clit in a quick pinch. Then pull.

I bucked under his touch. More. God. I was on the edge.

His command was sharp. "Come. Now."

He rubbed my clit hard and slipped two fingers inside me. My orgasm took on a life of its own. I clung to him, my arms wrapped around his head, holding him to me as pleasure made me lose all thought. I didn't know where I was, only that he was with me and that was the only thing that mattered.

When it was over, he did not speak, just put himself back together, grabbed a large towel, wrapped me up in it and grabbed my things. Once my pants and shoes were piled in my lap, he lifted me in his arms as he had done the day we met and carried me back to our quarters.

I rested my head on his shoulder, my body still languid and warm, and wondered if I'd just fallen in love with my third mate, or made the biggest mistake of my life?

eros

MAL WALKED in the door with Smith in his arms. She was wrapped in a towel from the training room. Her hair was a mess and her cheeks were flushed. Worse, she leaned into him like she could barely hold up her head.

"Is she hurt?"

"*She's* right here," Smith's voice sounded odd. I looked at Mal.

"What did you do?" I knew Mal would never truly harm a female, especially not one under his care. But the scenes that had played out at Club Trinity came to my mind. He had pushed her then. Perhaps this time he had pushed her too far.

"Nothing. She's fine."

"Then why is she crying?" I moved closer and leaned in to get a better look. I was correct, a small trail of dried salt was on her cheek. Her eyes were pink.

"*She's* right here. And *she's* not going to be discussed in the third person." She held up her hand but her tone softened. "Thank you, Geros. I'm okay."

I looked from her to Mal and gave up hope that I was going to get a better explanation.

The comm in our quarters chimed.

"Yes?" Kayson answered.

One of the three king's voices came through the comm. I never could tell them apart. "We have a lead on the traitor. We're moving out in two hours. Be ready."

The comm went dead and Smith wiggled in Mal's arms. Reluctantly, he set her down.

"That's good news, right? No more death threats. We take out the leadership and their organization crumbles. Peace on Viken at last?"

"Indeed." I did not want the mission to be over. I needed more time—*we* needed more time to woo her. Convince her to be ours, to stay.

"Okay. I guess I better get ready, too. We get the bad guys and then I guess I'll be going home." Her voice cracked on the word home, but she shook her head as if she were disagreeing with herself.

I would never understand females.

"Very well."

I watched her disappear inside her bedroom. Heard

the fall of water once the shower was turned on. I listened for the sound of her voice. She'd recently begun to sing a song to herself as she bathed. Listening was one of my guilty pleasures. But no sounds came through the door.

With a sigh I glanced over my shoulder to where Kayson sat on our sofa. "What are we going to do?" We were literally out of time.

"I don't know."

"Mal?"

His face was blank, as if his mind was very far away. "It's her choice. It has to be her choice."

Fuck. He was right. But if he had ruined our chance to have a family with Smith, I was going to strangle him with my bare hands.

Kayson shrugged and left to get our gear. Mal disappeared inside the other bedroom and started a second shower. Which left me standing alone in our living room.

Mal could be hard male to deal with, but he was our friend. Our brother in arms. He'd saved our lives too many times to count during the Hive war, just as we'd saved his.

But, if he didn't want Smith, I would find another male from Sector Two to take his place. Which meant he'd better pull his head out of his ass and realize how perfect Smith was in our lives. Fucking perfect. I didn't need an Interstellar Bride sent to me by some AI machine. Odds were, even if one of us did end up with a matched mate, two to one she would be matched to either Mal or Kayson, rather than me. How would that be any different than loving--and claiming--Smith?

I hadn't been able to stop thinking about the way she'd invited me to take her, fill her sweet ass. The way she bucked and demanded more, allowed me to claim her when she knew others watched. She'd given me a gift no female ever had. I'd been hers from that moment on.

Fuck. That was a lie. I'd wanted her from the moment I first saw her on the transport pad. Her dark hair. The curve of her hip. The fact that she was so outspoken, smart and courageous only added to my desire to claim her. She would be a wonderful mother. Would raise strong, happy children. I'd wanted a family since I was a boy but never found the right female. Now I had, and she was about to slip through my fingers.

My mate. Our mate. She was ours. Kayson was of similar mind. If Mal didn't come around, too fucking bad. I wasn't giving up this chance at happiness, at a future, because he was a stubborn fool.

When Kayson returned Mal was out of the shower and we all geared up together, as we had hundreds of times before. Smith's shower was still running, which meant we had a small window of time to talk without her hearing every word.

"What happened between you two today?" I asked.

Mal shrugged. "We had a disagreement. We argued, and then we settled it."

"What kind of disagreement?" Kayson was the one to push this time.

"It doesn't matter." Mal shoved one foot, then the other, into his boots. "I know you two want her to stay. You want to claim her."

I opened my mouth to make sure Mal knew exactly how much I wanted that to happen. But he raised his hand to stop me.

"I know you want her. She's intelligent, fearless, beautiful, passionate—"

"Why do I hear a but coming?" Kayson tucked his ion blaster into its holster and stared at Mal. We were both staring at him, waiting for him to explain himself.

"But...she's not an Interstellar Bride. We have no legal claim on her, no leverage and no rights." Mal reached for his own blaster and secured it to his uniform. "Has she said one word, one single word to either one of you, indicating she wants to stay on Viken at all? Or be with us long term? Has she slipped into our beds these past nights?"

No. The answer was no, to all of it. She hadn't said a single word to make me think she wanted to stay on Viken. There had been four nights when she could have asked one, or all of us, to sleep next to her, or hold her, or fuck her. Instead, she'd disappeared into her room and closed the door, locking us out.

Mal's words were harsh, but true. Perhaps she didn't want us at all. Was she counting down the moment until she would return to Earth and get her promotion? And although she'd let me take her body, fill her and take pleasure from her, she had not once taken us together.

Not two of us, and definitely not all three. Perhaps she had no desire to do so. Ever.

Or perhaps we just needed to ask.

————

SMITH

THE HOT WATER cascaded down my body, washing the tears from my eyes. The warmth was comforting, like a hug; the heat seeping into my skin and easing tense muscles. I could smell the shampoo I had used earlier and feel my wet hair clinging to my back. I could smell Mal in the steam rising up from the shower as the water washed him away. The droplets on my face washing away the small bit of blush I'd applied before tracking Mal down. I'd wanted to look good. Healthy. Strong.

Not the broken-hearted creature I felt like inside.

The pitter-patter of the water against the tiled walls kept me company. I could hear the guys talking, but I didn't try to make out the words. I was afraid to know. For the first time in years, I had let myself be vulnerable.

And now it was over. We were about to flush out the big bad guy, the head of the serpent. Take the VSS out once and for all.

It was a huge success. A boon for my career.

So why was I so miserable?

I stood there, letting the hot water wash over me,

trying to clear my mind. I had just had a breakthrough with Mal. Kayson and Geros were keepers as well. All three of them were protective and sexy and each one of them so perfect for me.

I washed the last of Mal from my body and nearly started crying again.

Instead, I closed my eyes and reminded myself that I was a federal agent. I was sent here to do a job, and I was determined to see it through. I had to focus on that, not on my feelings or what-ifs. Once those two adorable little girls were safe, I'd deal with my personal problems. Work first.

Put it away, Carmen. Focus, or you'll get yourself killed.

I slowly opened my eyes and tried to push away the storm of emotion rolling around inside me, knocking me off balance. I had to focus on the moment. One thing at a time. That was how I kept going. One step at a time. One hour at a time. One day at a time. One problem at a time.

Now's problem was the VSS and only the VSS.

I stepped out of the shower, my legs trembling as I thought about the three males waiting for me to walk out of this room. Kayson with his wicked tongue, his soft lips and his gentleness when I needed someone to hold me. Geros with his solid strength, his total loyalty and commitment to family. The way he'd felt filling my ass, hands on my hips wrapping his fingers around me like he never wanted to let go. The tender kiss he'd given me after.

And Mal. Silent, stubborn Mal. Always giving others

what they needed and taking nothing for himself. He'd pushed me out of a sexual box that I would never be able to fit into again. He'd pushed me and I'd pushed back. Today. I'd broken down one of his walls, just as he'd broken down mine.

I froze for a moment consumed by the memory of his body on top of me as he filled me from behind. The way his heat had closed in around me. The sting of his hand on my bottom as I'd pushed him for more and more and more.

I took one lazy step and the coldness of the smooth floor was a shock after the warmth of the cascading water. I shivered as I made my way to the sink. Wrapping myself in a fresh towel, I looked at my reflection in the mirror and didn't recognize the woman staring back at me.

She looked exactly the same as the woman who'd arrived on this planet. Same face. Same hair. Same eyes. But inside, behind those eyes, everything was different.

I had so many questions and not enough answers. I felt like I was chasing ghosts, and the more I tried to understand my guys, the farther away they seemed to be.

THE PALACE GARDENS, usually a place of solace and beauty, sent a chill through me now. Darkness had fallen. The tall trees seemed to whisper warnings, and the lush grass was stained with a reddish hue. The stunning flowerbeds, a riot of color and life, became a blur as I moved, hunting our prey.

I had been patrolling the royal palace for years. I did not care for politicians and their games and so I had paid no attention to them. Still, I never felt comfortable around this particular council member.

Vikter was considered not just a close friend, but an ally of the queen's on all political matters. She trusted him implicitly. And he had betrayed us all, tried to murder the queen and the kings' daughter. He was responsible for riots and protests, attacks and disruption to peoples' lives in all three sectors of Viken. He was the leader of the Viken Sector Separatists, and he'd been sitting at the royal family's dinner table nearly every night for years.

Apparently, Vikter wanted things to be the way they'd always been. Decades of war had made his family very, very wealthy. Powerful. Influential. Without a war to fight, his voice faded in importance and the money dried up.

I had been waiting in the garden to catch him meeting with some VSS members, but it was proving to be more difficult than we had anticipated. The meeting that was supposed to take place was now nearly an hour overdue. There were multiple people working to catch him in the act and document the entire event. I was here in case he made a run for it. One of us was stationed in every direction to head him off and arrest him.

If he ever showed up.

Either Vikter been tipped off, or the meeting had been canceled.

My heart jumped at the thought. Vikter was powerful. The royal family needed irrefutable evidence to take him down. Without this meeting, they wouldn't have it. Not yet. They would have to plot and plan and wait for the perfect moment to strike.

Which meant Smith would stay a little while longer.

I had tried to keep my distance, to do the honorable thing and keep my hands to myself. And what now? I was afraid I was in love with her, just like Kayson and Geros. Which meant we would all have our hearts broken together when Smith left us behind.

Had I been foolish not to tell Smith I wanted to be with her before leaving our quarters tonight?

But she'd come out of her bedroom dressed in armor, like a fighter. She even had a weapon in a holster on her side. When I'd begun to say something, the look she gave me was pure irritated female. I kept my mouth shut.

But where was she now? The three kings as well as Kayson, Geros and I were spread out on the massive palace grounds with at least a dozen other guards, hiding in all the darkest places, waiting for Vikter and his VSS sympathizers to show themselves.

I had assumed Smith would be out here, with us, where I could keep an eye on her. But the queen had taken her away from the group the moment we'd arrived and I hadn't seen her since.

A shout rang out in the distance, followed by blaster fire. The comms blew up as guards reported in. Two explosions, on opposite ends of the grounds. A grove of trees in yet another area was on fire, threatening to spread toward the palace. Teams were racing to put it out. And in all the noise and chatter, there was one voice I did not hear.

Where was Smith?

I raced past the marble statues and fountains, the cobblestone path a blur beneath my feet as I ran to assist the nearest group.

I rounded the corner, and the scene in front of me was a nightmare. Males and females scattered around, some lying on the ground, and others standing still in shock. My heart plunged as I saw Smith in the center of it all, her pale face looking around with pure rage. She didn't appear to be harmed. I stumbled forward, and several people looked up at me in relief.

I only cared about one of them.

"Are you unharmed?" I grabbed Smith's elbow and tugged until she looked up at me. When she didn't respond, I tried again. "Smith! Talk to me. Are you hurt?"

"No." She turned her head, looking around once more, doing some kind of strange calculation I couldn't seem to get out of her. "This was all a set-up. A trap. But why?" She glanced back at the palace and her face went pale. "Oh, god. The queen. The girls!"

She took off at a dead run, surprisingly fast for someone so small.

The sound of the palace alarms blared into the gardens, adding to the chaos and confusion.

"What does that sound mean?" Smith yelled the question as she ran headfirst into danger. Without thought to her own safety. Without fear. I saw her as she truly was for the first time, a warrior. A fighter I would proudly stand next to. I couldn't lie to her.

"Nothing good."

———

SMITH

THE CHAOS inside the palace was worse than outside. Staff ran everywhere asking questions. No one knew why the alarm had been activated. No one could find the queen—or her daughters. Several guards had been found unconscious on the floor outside the royal family's private quarters. The three kings were on their way back to the palace.

No one knew anything and everyone was panicked.

Typical. People were people, no matter what planet they were on.

I grabbed one of the staff, a young man who seemed relatively calm. "What's the fastest route to the queen's bedroom?"

"She isn't there. We looked. We already looked." He looked confused, like his own words didn't make sense.

"And Allayna? Lilliana?"

He shook his head. "No. It's empty. No one is there."

Shit. I looked at Mal. "Do you think he kidnapped them? Took them for leverage or ransom?"

Mal shook his head. "No. We know who he is now. He has nothing to gain by allowing them to live. If he'd found them in their rooms, they'd already be dead."

Comforting. "Is there any way to get on or off this island quietly? Without being noticed?"

Mal considered, then shook his head. "No. The docks are monitored by satellite as well as manned stations. No ships are allowed to fly overhead. It's one of the reasons this was chosen as the capital."

"Then they must still be here. Somewhere. Where would she go?" Where would I go with two scared little girls? Somewhere a bad guy would most likely never think to look.

And then I knew.

"Mal! Follow me! Come on! I think I know where they are."

Mal fell in behind me, as did several others who had been standing around the foyer looking lost. Good. If we were going to run into VSS goons I'd take all the help I could get.

Cornered rats were dangerous. They had nothing to lose.

When we got close to the throne room, I put up my fist in the air and hoped they would all know what that meant. Stop. Be quiet. Wait.

Mal and I moved to opposite sides of the door. We made eye contact and understood one another perfectly. "On three," I whispered.

I did a silent countdown with three fingers and we moved in, checking the corners, covering each other's backs.

"Clear." I gave the signal and the rest of the guards who'd come with us moved inside. I looked them over. They would do.

Mal must have agreed with my assessment. "Guard

that door. No one comes in unless it's the three kings themselves. Understood?"

They accepted Mal's command and moved into place, most likely glad to have an assignment, something to do. I tilted my head toward the private garden where I'd met the queen and Lilliana before. This area was separate from the sprawl of the main grounds—grounds that were now on fire. This was meant to be a personal sanctuary, a safe place for the royal children to play. Tall walls enclosed the large space. It was basically the royal family's private park and was more than large enough to hide a woman and two little girls.

Mal and I approached quietly.

"Don't freak her out. She's probably armed and ready to shoot anything that moves." I would be, if it were my children I was protecting from lunatics who wanted them dead.

Speaking of, I pulled my Glock from its holster and held it in ready position.

"Leah? It's me." I called out into the darkness several times as I followed one of the garden paths. Each time, I made my voice a bit louder. "Leah? Are you out here? We've got the throne room secured. Mal is with me. Are you here? You can come out now."

There was a quiet rustle of leaves.

I moved closer. "Leah?"

"I'm afraid not." A tall Viken male stood up slowly. He was much older than Mal, but still moved like he was a trained fighter. Gray hair and a few wrinkles didn't fool me. Sometime the older ones were the meanest. They had to be. They'd lived longer than everyone else around them, and it wasn't by accident.

"I assume you're Vikter?" I still had my pistol in my hand, the weapon their S-Gen machine had blessed me with right after I arrived. It was black, not shiny and silver like the ion blasters. I put the weapon down along my thigh and angled my body away from him, hoping he wouldn't see it.

"And you are the annoying bitch from Earth the queen set about sniffing at my heels."

I'd been called worse things than a dog. Much worse. His words didn't concern me, it was the blaster pointed at the center of my chest. No dodging that.

"Leah, if you're here, hide! Don't come out," I shouted, much louder than anything I'd yelled out before.

"Silence!" He glared at me, the hatred in his gaze a living, breathing thing. "Earth. Pitiful little planet. And yet here you are. Another arrogant female from Earth who thinks she can change the world. *My* world."

"Is this where you do your super long, villain monologue?" I feigned a yawn.

He looked confused. "Are you insane?"

He was asking *me* that question? "Last I checked, you were the one trying to kill helpless little girls."

Where was Mal? I knew he had been behind me when I came in here. Like, *right behind me.*

All I could do was keep stalling.

I glanced to the side and saw something that made my heart leap into my throat.

No.

The queen and her daughters were there, hiding in the foliage not three steps away from us. Three steps away from this maniac and his blaster. Shit.

"They should never have been conceived."

"Well, that's one opinion." I took a step back, away from the queen, in the hopes crazy-killer-man would walk with me. No such luck. I was going to have to take my shot and hope for the best.

Mal was close, I knew he was.

"Why are you in here, Vikter?"

"The same reason you are, searching for the queen and her daughters."

"I guess we're both losers then, aren't we?"

"Some more than others. Good-bye human." He lifted the blaster just a hint, a mere twitch of his hand really.

It was enough. I dropped to my knee and rolled to my side, just like I'd done hundreds of times in training. When I came up out of the roll, I was already shooting.

My gun was loud. So damn loud after the quiet hiss and buzz of the ion blasters.

Old school, but efficient.

Vikter stared down at his chest in shock as a blood-stain spread like spilled water on his chest.

The humming energy of an ion blaster firing several shots whizzed by my head from behind. Three Viken males screamed in pain and crashed into the bushes in front of me. I hadn't seen them, but they'd been there the whole time, hiding behind Vikter.

Mal.

So that's where you've been.

I turned to see him climbing down from...something. A tree? I couldn't quite make it out in the dim light. He walked past me and kicked all four dead males for good measure.

"Are we good?" I asked.

"Yes. I found no more of Vikter's soldiers in this garden."

I turned to where the queen was hiding. "You can come out now." I pointed to a path that would keep the little ones away from the dead bodies. "I'd come out over there and keep the princesses on that side of the garden."

Leah moved through the underbrush in the direction I'd told her to go. Once there, she stood, Allayna clutching her skirt, staying close. Lilliana, however, had a yellow flower in her hand and walked straight up to me with her gift. I bent down and took it. "Thank you. Such a pretty yellow flower."

The little one smiled and went back to her mother.

"It was Vikter all right, " the queen said. "Him and half the council. They showed up and tried to tear down the doors to my room."

"How did you get out?" I asked.

She grinned like she was a kid herself. "Secret passage."

"Cool."

"The kings will want names." Mal moved to stand behind me, covering my back. I noticed. So sweet.

And names? Yes. More like blood types so they could keep the council members aligned with the VSS alive and torture them longer.

Or maybe that was just me thinking about them hurting these adorable little girls.

Allayna stared at me. I smiled back.

"Are you a fighter, like my dads?"

"Yes, I am."

"I didn't know girls could be fighters."

"Well, they can," I assured her.

Behind us the guards we'd left in the throne room were making their way out to check on us after all the noise. Mal went back to talk to them. He took care of it quickly and efficiently and returned to my side. I could get used to having him there.

Allayna smiled at me, tugged on her mother's skirt and waited for Leah to look down into her sweet, innocent face. "Momma, I'm going to be a fighter when I grow up."

The queen told her that would be just fine and waited for her to scamper off with her little sister, far away from Vikter and his minions. Then she inspected me, top to bottom, boots to armor and the gun in-between. "Oh, dear. What have you done?"

Next to me, Mal burst out laughing.

16

S *mith, Viken United, The Palace*

FIRST, there was a feast. A real royal feast with a table that felt like it was a block long and more food than I'd ever seen in one place. Music. Entertainers. Dancers. The VSS had finally been snuffed out and the mood in the room was happy. Contagious.

Except for the fact that I was packed and leaving for Earth as soon as it was over. Worse, I hadn't seen any of my guys since the night before. They'd each given me a hug and said goodnight. When I woke up this morning, they were gone.

I'd thought, after the day with Mal, after giving myself to Kayson and Geros, that maybe they would say something or do something to indicate they cared about me. Wanted me to stay and be with them. Anything.

I'd waited in vain. Vikter had been dead for two days. It was time to cut my losses and go before it hurt any worse. As if that were possible.

The three kings stood as one, striking their goblets with their royal rings, making a clatter.

"Ladies and gentlemen, esteemed guests, we would like to honor a very special person this night." They all turned and looked at me.

Me?

"Ms. Smith, from Earth, the investigator who has finally brought an end to the VSS and the threat to Viken's future."

The entire room erupted in applause and loud cheers. My face, I knew, was hot pink and getting redder by the second. Queen Leah walked around the table and took my hand. Once she had ahold of me, she dragged me up to the dais with the four thrones and pushed me down on hers. "Sit."

"What?"

She just shook her head and smiled at me as the three kings clinked their rings against their goblets again and the room quieted.

"We have a surprise for her, for all of you." One of the kings spoke, I wasn't sure which one he was, other than he was the one with a scar on his face. And Lilliana was curled up, bottom on his forearm, head nestled in his shoulder watching the activity as Allayna sat between the other two kings in her own special chair. The whole family was glowing. And I'd helped do that. I'd done good. But if I'd known Leah was going to put me in this chair with the whole room watching I might have chosen to wear something other than black pants and a blouse. Maybe some heels? A bit of make-up at least?

A large door opened slowly. Standing on the other side were Mal, Geros and Kayson in their sector colors, brown, black and steel gray, red bands around their biceps, signifying they were royal guards. They were gorgeous. Sexy. And looking up at me. On a throne that was not mine, on a planet that was not mine.

But I wanted it to be.

They walked forward side-by-side until they stood before me. Then? They kneeled like knights in front of a queen.

"My lady, we know you did not choose us," Mal began.

"But we have chosen you. We offer ourselves as your mates." Geros dared look up at me, just a bit. The love and hope I saw in his eyes took my breath away.

Kayson looked up at me as well. "If you will have us, we will devote ourselves to you from this day until our last days."

I looked at Leah. "What do I do?" Was I supposed to bow or say some weird words or what?

She smiled. "Say yes."

———

I FELT LIKE A GODDESS, a powerful, desirable ruler of men.

These men. MY men. Well, aliens from another planet with magical semen, but they were still mine.

And now they were the only people on this planet who knew my real name. I couldn't claim them and let them think my name really was Smith.

No, when they groaned in pleasure or Mal gave me a naughty order, I wanted to hear my own name. Carmen. And not that bitchy, internal critic's version of my name.

From their lips it would be sexy. Erotic.

"By the gods, you are perfect." Kayson's words were torn from his throat as he kissed his way from my lips to my bare breasts. Lower.

Geros and Mal both nodded agreement as they watched. Both of them liked to watch.

"Kiss her, Kayson. Everywhere, just like you want to. Fill that hot mouth of hers with your cock. Geros, her ass is yours. Make sure she's ready."

"Fuck, Mal. I knew you were going to start giving orders," Geros complained, but he was grinning as he did so, moving next to me on the sofa and turning me to the side so Mal could grab my wrists. Mal's strong hands wrapped around my wrists and my insides melted. I was under his control now. I didn't have to think any more. I could just feel.

He held them in place behind my back as Kayson worked his way from my hard nipples to my clit. He moved his tongue over me, inside me. He sucked the sensitive nub as I leaned into Mal's hold with a soft groan.

"She likes that, Kayson. Suck that swollen clit right into your mouth. Play with her." Mal liked to give orders. Restrained, pussy wet, I knew that if I were a good girl, I'd tell them to stop.

But I was done with that old version of myself, of my former life. I'd resigned my job on Earth and taken a new one as the queen's personal assistant. Which basically meant I got to run around and stick my nose in everyone's business, find out what was going on. Learn everyone's secrets. Take a special interest where the queen wanted me to. It was perfect.

And then it was nothing because Geros's hands cupped my bare breasts. Mal's commanding grip on my wrists reminded me that I was theirs now, theirs to conquer, theirs to fuck, and that knowledge broke me open. Raw need flooded every cell of my body. I moaned. I couldn't hold it in. Was my life really going to be this simple?

Yes. The answer was a song inside me as Mal tied my wrists and moved to stand in front of me. His gaze lingered, a hot caress everywhere it touched. Yes. I was theirs. They were mine. They were going to give me what I needed, even when I wasn't exactly sure what that was anymore. They would take care of me. Protect me.

Love me.

And I knew what I needed. Them. I needed my mates. Like this. Naked. Surrounding me. Home. I was home.

———

KAYSON

GEROS CLIMBED up on the bed behind her. He tugged her hair with his free hand and angled her head, exposing her neck for his kiss. He kicked her legs wide and she fell back against his bare chest, completely under his control. Trusting us, all of us to take her, to fuck her, claim her. Make her ours forever.

As Mal watched, I leaned forward and licked her pussy, lingering on the hard nub of her clit. She whimpered as I played, her taste an addiction I would never break.

I ran my tongue over her, hard and rough, marking her, making her mine as I was hers. As I would always belong to her.

"Fill her up, Geros. I want to make her come." I wanted my mouth on her pussy as Geros fucked her ass and filled her up. My command drew a whimper from her.

"Do you want them to stop?" Mal asked the question. Geros and I froze, waiting for her answer. I didn't want to stop, but I would, in a heartbeat, if that was what she wanted.

"No. Don't stop. I want all of you."

Her soft confession was also a clear demand from our new mate, one we would not deny.

I lowered my head to her once more, feasting on her

wet heat. On the female I loved. The one who was mine. Forever and always mine.

———

GEROS

Kayson's order to fill our mate's ass made my cock jump as if Kayson spoke directly to it. Pre-cum leaked from the tip as I slipped a small lube tablet inside our mate's pretty bottom. Her wrists were tied behind her back, her legs spread open wide over my thighs. Kayson had his head buried in her pussy and her ass, her soft, sweet backside was already in my lap.

I moaned, long, loud and demanding, not caring if the others heard me. This was our female, our mate. Desiring her was a privilege.

I kissed her neck once more and nibbled on her ear as I placed my cock at her tight entrance. "I'm going to fuck you now. Your ass is mine. Your body is mine. You're going to take all of me, mate. Every fucking inch."

Her breathing hitched and she leaned her head back into me, putting more weight on my chest. Choosing me.

I pressed my cock into her slowly, gently. I didn't want to hurt her, I wanted to claim her. Love her. She was my family now, this was my family and she meant everything.

When I was balls deep, I nodded at Mal.

Kayson's mouth left her pussy and she whimpered in protest. He gave her no time to recover, moving to suck one nipple into his mouth. We'd talked to Mal, we'd both been in that room with her in the club. Kayson gave her a little bite with his teeth and her ass clenched so tightly I worried she might make me come now.

Drugged on sensation, I glanced down to watch him, to see how his mouth moved over her. I cupped her breasts and held them up for him, playing with one nipple as he suckled on the other. I loved how we looked together as we pleasured our mate.

"Beautiful," Mal said watching from where he stood next to her hip, his voice thick with lust. "The picture of perfect submission."

I lifted my hips, fucking her, moving in and out of her ass. "Geros. Oh, God."

She moaned, arching her back, straining against the rope binding her wrists, pressing against Kayson's tongue.

Fuck. I had to stop. I was going to come and come hard. Not yet. Not fucking yet. Not until we were all inside her, until the claiming was complete.

"Mal, you're next," I said as I withdrew. "Hurry." The strained sound of my voice made both Mal and Kayson chuckle, but they weren't inside her, the pleasure so intense it bordered on pain. And love only made the feelings stronger.

Mal

She was nearly there. I'd seen her like this before and

I hoped to see her like this for the rest of my life. She was beautiful. Perfect.

Mine.

I would share her with Geros and Kayson because it was what she wanted, what they wished for as well. But in the dark places in my heart, she was mine. She'd given herself to me and I was not letting her go.

"Please," she moaned, needing more.

Kayson looked up at me from where he now had his face pressed against her thigh. "Ready to join in the fun?"

"Mal." She begged, my name on her lips like a whip to my cock. I was engorged. In pain. My balls ready to burst. For her. Only for her.

"My cock is yours, mate" Geros said. He shifted slightly, make more room for me to fuck her from the front, to fill her pussy the way he was balls deep in her ass. He pulled her ass cheeks wide and her pussy opened up like a flower.

Her head dropped back on his shoulder and she moaned. Said my name again.

"Yes," I answered, not exactly sure what she was asking. Yes, was my answer. It was always going to be my answer.

"Tell me what you want, mate."

Mate, that word. She was mine. "I want you inside me. I want all three of you."

"That's not the way you speak to me, mate." I pushed two fingers into her pussy, making sure she was wet. Ready.

"Sir. I want you inside me, Sir. Please."

"Good girl," I gave her praise because I knew she liked to hear the words. But I also gave her what she needed. Completion. A claiming.

I slid by cock into her wet heat. Geros groaned, the size of my cock putting pressure on his.

"Yes." She thrashed her head from side to side.

With one hard thrust I entered her completely, not stopping until I was as deep as she could take me. She gasped, then moaned

I couldn't help myself, I had to tell her. I'd tell her every day. "I love you, Carmen. I love you."

———

CARMEN

THERE WERE TWO OF THEM, two cocks inside me, tugging at me, two different styles, two different ways of moving. One was gentle, calm and smooth, the other dark, powerful and commanding. One was in control and one yielded to me. That's what it was like. But I needed to make this claiming complete. Two wasn't enough. I wanted all of them.

They. Were. Mine.

"I love all of you. You're all mine. I need you. All of you."

With one lover fucking my pussy and another buried

deeply in my ass, I turned my head to the side and licked my lips--*slowly.* I beckoned Kayson to bring his huge cock closer so I could take him into my mouth. I wanted to fuck all three of them. I needed them to be as insane with pleasure as I was. And to do that, I needed to wrap my lips and tongue around Kayson's hard length.

I licked the head and felt his gasp against the top of my head. I licked down one side and then the other, savoring the way the salty pre-cum from his tip tingled in my mouth. I swept my tongue along the thick vein on the underside of his cock, then flicked it back and forth against the tip.

I needed to taste each of them. I needed to feel them inside me, all of us, together, until we exploded in ecstasy.

"That's it, mate," Mal growled. "Take all of us."

I purred against Kayson's cock, my voice vibrating along its thick length. Kayson let out a little growl, his fingers tangling in my hair. I wanted to make him as crazy as I was.

My head bobbed up and down, sucking and licking and teasing until Kayson was so big and hard that it was almost impossible to open wide enough to take him. I wanted him to lose control. I wanted to own his pleasure the way he'd dictated mine with his wicked, wicked tongue.

The rhythm of his breathing changed, and I wrapped my lips around his cock once more, pulling him into my mouth and swirling my tongue around the head. I fucked his cock with my mouth in a rhythm to match the other two moving deep inside of me. I looked up at his face and saw him swallow hard, his gaze glued to my body, to the places Mal and Geros moved in and out of me.

I loved how their bodies reacted to me, almost as if they had no say in the matter. I wanted to pleasure them all so much that none of my mates would ever look at another woman and want her. The only woman they would ever think of like this was me.

Mine. He was mine. Just like Mal and Geros were mine.

As if he knew I was thinking about him, Mal grabbed a fistful of my hair and pulled back against my head's movements. "You love how big Kayson is?" Mal whispered as he continued to fuck my pussy while Geros worked himself in and out of my ass. "You love how my cock is so deep inside you? Do you love Geros's cock buried in your ass?"

Hell to the yeah, but I couldn't say the words. My mouth was kinda full.

"Do you want me to fuck you harder? Do you want to feel me slam against your clit?"

As Mal teased me with dirty talk, Geros massaged my bottom and thighs. Pulling. Rubbing. Just right.

God, these guys were lethal. My body had no problem with that, my back arching off Geros's chest. I moaned around Kayson's cock, grinding my hips against Mal to get more friction. I was beyond thought, I was an animal and I needed to come.

Geros reached up on my left side, took one hard nipple between his fingers and tugged. At the same time, he used his other hand to swat my bottom just hard enough for it to sting.

Holy shit.

I was gone, my orgasm a living, breathing thing that gobbled me up and spit me out. This was more intense than anything we'd ever done before and I knew it was because they were truly mine now. This was the claiming, the moment I realized there was never going to be a time in my future when I would be alone. Unloved.

And neither would they. I would take care of them just like they would care for me.

Kayson's cock pulsed in my mouth and I swallowed him down. I wanted all of him, just like I wanted everything from my other two mates. Perhaps it was my pleasure that pushed them over, or seeing Kayson give in to his orgasm, but Mal and Geros thrust just that smallest bit harder. Deeper. Then they were filling me with their seed as well.

Magical semen. No lie, the heat of the chemicals that gave the Viken their infamous "Seed Power" didn't hit me like a punch--as it had the first time. No, this time the heat melted into my bones, into my blood. Into my heart.

I wanted them again...and I always would.

A SPECIAL THANK YOU TO MY READERS...

Want more? I've got **hidden** bonus content on my web site *exclusively* for those on my <u>mailing list.</u>

If you are already on my email list, you don't need to do a thing! Simply scroll to the bottom of my newsletter emails and click on the **super-secret** link.

Not a member? What are you waiting for? In addition to bonus content (great new stuff will be added regularly) you will always be in the loop - you'll never have to wonder when my newest release will hit the stores—AND you will get a free book as a special welcome gift.

Sign up now! http://freescifiromance.com

FIND YOUR INTERSTELLAR MATCH!

YOUR mate is out there. Take the test today and discover your perfect match. Are you ready for a sexy alien mate (or two)?

VOLUNTEER NOW!

interstellarbridesprogram.com

DO YOU LOVE AUDIOBOOKS?

Grace Goodwin's books are now available as
audiobooks...everywhere.

LET'S TALK!

Interested in joining my **Sci-Fi Squad**? Meet new like-minded sci-fi romance fanatics and chat with Grace! Be part of a private Facebook group that shares pictures and fun news! Join here:

https://www.facebook.com/groups/scifisquad/

Want to talk about Grace Goodwin books with others? Join the **SPOILER ROOM** and spoil away! Your GG BFFs are waiting! (And so is Grace) Join here:

https://www.facebook.com/groups/ggspoilerroom/

GET A FREE BOOK!

JOIN MY MAILING LIST TO BE THE FIRST TO KNOW OF NEW RELEASES, FREE BOOKS, SPECIAL PRICES AND OTHER AUTHOR GIVEAWAYS.

http://freescifiromance.com

ALSO BY GRACE GOODWIN

Surprise Mates

Rogue Enforcer

Chosen by the Vikens

Interstellar Brides® Program Boxed Set - Books 6-8

Interstellar Brides® Program Boxed Set - Books 9-12

Interstellar Brides® Program Boxed Set - Books 13-16

Interstellar Brides® Program Boxed Set - Books 17-20

Bad Boys of Rogue 5

Interstellar Brides® Program: The Colony

Surrender to the Cyborgs

Mated to the Cyborgs

Cyborg Seduction

Her Cyborg Beast

Cyborg Fever

Rogue Cyborg

Cyborg's Secret Baby

Her Cyborg Warriors

Claimed by the Cyborgs

The Colony Boxed Set 1

The Colony Boxed Set 2

The Colony Boxed Set 3

Interstellar Brides® Program: The Virgins

The Alien's Mate

His Virgin Mate

Claiming His Virgin

His Virgin Bride

His Virgin Princess

The Virgins - Complete Boxed Set

Interstellar Brides® Program: Ascension Saga

Ascension Saga, book 1

Ascension Saga, book 2

Ascension Saga, book 3

Trinity: Ascension Saga - Volume 1

Ascension Saga, book 4

Ascension Saga, book 5

Ascension Saga, book 6

Faith: Ascension Saga - Volume 2

Ascension Saga, book 7

Ascension Saga, book 8

Ascension Saga, book 9

Destiny: Ascension Saga - Volume 3

Interstellar Brides® Program: The Beasts

Bachelor Beast

Maid for the Beast

Beauty and the Beast

The Beasts Boxed Set - Books 1-3

Big Bad Beast

Beast Charming

Bargain with a Beast

The Beasts Boxed Set - Books 4-6

Starfighter Training Academy

The First Starfighter

Starfighter Command

Elite Starfighter

Starfighter Training Academy Boxed Set

Other Books

Dragon Chains

Their Conquered Bride

Wild Wolf Claiming: A Howl's Romance

SUBSCRIBE TODAY!

Hi there! Grace Goodwin here. I am SO excited to invite you into my intense, crazy, sexy, romantic, imagination and the worlds born as a result. From Battlegroup Karter to The Colony and on behalf of the entire Coalition Fleet of Planets, I welcome you! Visit my Patreon page for additional bonus content, sneak peaks, and insider information on upcoming books as well as the opportunity to receive NEW RELEASE BOOKS before anyone else! See you there! ~ Grace

Grace's PATREON: https://www.patreon.com/gracegoodwin

ABOUT GRACE

Grace Goodwin is a USA Today and international bestselling author of Sci-Fi and Paranormal romance with over a million books sold. Grace's titles are available worldwide on all retailers, in multiple languages, and in ebook, print, audio and other reading App formats.

Grace is a full-time writer whose earliest movie memories are of Luke Skywalker, Han Solo, and real, working light sabers. (Still waiting for Santa to come through on that one.) Now Grace writes sexy-as-hell sci-fi romance six days a week. In her spare time, she reads, watches campy sci-fi and enjoys spending time with family and friends. No matter where she is, there is always a part of her dreaming up new worlds and exciting characters for her next book.

Grace loves to chat with readers and can frequently be found lurking in her Facebook groups. Interested in joining her **Sci-Fi Squad**? Meet new like-minded sci-fi romance fanatics and chat with Grace! Join here: https://www.facebook.com/groups/scifisquad/

Want to talk about Grace Goodwin books with others? Join the **SPOILER ROOM** and spoil away! Your GG BFFs are waiting! (And so is Grace) Join here:

https://www.facebook.com/groups/ggspoilerroom/

Printed in Great Britain
by Amazon

20589055R00122